At the end of the first verse, there was a break in the music. When Leanne came to that part, she stopped, just like Lara did on the record. She counted three beats in her head. One . . . two . . . But as she was taking her breath to resume the song, she heard a squeal of laughter explode in the auditorium.

"Maybe Leanne should put out a rock video," one girl giggled sarcastically.

"Only if she shaved her head," said the other.

"Who would notice? She already looks so spooky."

Leanne knew those voices well. It was Lisa Avery and Brandy Kurtz.

**Look for this and other books in the
TOTALLY HOT series:**

point

TOTALLY HOT

#3 Standing Alone

Linda A. Cooney

SCHOLASTIC INC.
New York Toronto London Auckland Sydney

ISBN 0-590-44562-6

12 11 10 9 8 7 6 5 4 3 2 1   1 2 3 4 5 6/9

Printed in the U.S.A.   01

First Scholastic printing, December 1991

ONE

Leanne Heard's dishwashing shift was over.

She was alone in the Tucker Resort employee dressing room. Work had been crazy. Crescent Bay was having an unseasonable hot spell, and the resort was packed. It was after nine P.M. and guests were still pouring off the beach and into the dining rooms. Even though it was a fall Tuesday, it felt like a crowded weekend in the middle of July.

"Crowds," Leanne muttered.

Leanne peeled her damp T-shirt off her pale, sticky skin. but it wasn't easy. Her lace bra, bought recently at a secondhand store, stuck to her and chafed. Desperate to get cool, Leanne stretched out on the floor for a moment. She propped up her feet on the dressing room bench, then lay backward. The hard, cool concrete felt good beneath her back, and the overhead fan created a soft breeze that touched her bare shoulders.

That's when Leanne heard someone outside the door. She immediately scrambled back up to the bench again, sat down, and rested her face in her hands. Finally she stood up and stretched her arms over her head. She would have to deal with the tourists when she walked home. She couldn't always avoid crowds, so she simply cut through them. That had been her policy for a long time, and it had certainly helped her survive as a junior at Crescent Bay High.

Ffffttt. Ffffttt. Ffffttt.

The overhead fan continued to flip around, and Leanne closed her eyes. She hummed to herself as she lifted her dyed platinum hair and let her head fall forward, exposing her bare neck to the circulating air.

Nice.

Since Leanne had left her mother's house and moved into a crummy rented room, there hadn't been much niceness in her life. That was okay. She'd never trusted niceness anyway. She figured it was only a cover for something else. Still, when niceness came along in rare moments like this, it was hard to resist enjoying it a little.

Concentrating on the cooling breeze, Leanne didn't move, even though she was dimly aware that someone had opened the dressing-room door. She heard the squeaky footsteps of rubber-soled shoes and assumed that it was a waitress or a maid. Leanne sang softly, losing herself for a moment in a song that had played all night on the kitchen radio. She often sang to herself, so that she wouldn't have to talk to people. But then she felt the breeze turn warmer, and realized that a person had crept up close behind her and was blowing on the back of her neck.

"Not only does she wash dishes," a male voice whispered, each word sending a short puff against her skin, "but she sings, too."

"HEY!" Leanne let her hair fall to her bare shoulders as she spun around and jumped back. When she saw that it was Brent Tucker, every muscle in her hot, tired body grew tense. She looked around. The dressing room was still almost empty. Just her, Brent, the lockers, and the walls.

She flung one arm over her bra and the other across her bare middle. "Do you mind!" she cried, cringing and turning away.

"I was just looking for a place to hang out," Brent explained.

"Great," she spat back. "This is the women's dressing room."

Brent shrugged. He didn't look impressed. He was the son of the people who owned the resort. He was also a Crescent Bay High junior, but that was about the only thing he and Leanne had in common. Brent's family was rich. Leanne didn't really even have a family, and they certainly had no money. Brent had just moved to the small town of Crescent Bay. Leanne had been born in the town. Most people at school were in awe of Brent. They gossiped and snickered about Leanne. Finally, most kids thought Brent looked perfect with his blond hair and strong features. Leanne knew that most people didn't look at her — period.

Brent sat on the bench, making it hard for Leanne to miss his bare, sunburned chest. He was wearing white shorts and court shoes, with a while polo shirt stuck in his waistband and a tennis racket dangling from his hand. His back was smooth and muscular, with one white scar across the meaty part of his shoulder. All that white was in stark contrast to his blue eyes and ruddy tanned face.

"Do you always hang out here?" Leanne challenged.

Brent wiped his forehead with his wristband. He took in her pale skin and baggy, parachute pants. "Don't be so nervous. It's nothing I haven't seen before."

Leanne decided to take him up on his Mr. Experienced dare, sensing that her modesty only gave him more power. Reminding herself that a bra was no different from a bathing suit top, she relaxed her arms and leaned back against the lockers, then tried not to tremble when he stared as if she were a movie he'd rented for the night.

"Take a picture, why don't you," Leanne muttered.

Brent laughed and finally put his head down. Dropping a tennis ball, he began bouncing it with his racket. "Sorry. I know I shouldn't have come in here, but I looked first and I knew you weren't naked or anything. I was just thinking about something."

"Gee, thanks. Now I'm a thing."

"What?"

"You said you were thinking about something. Am I the 'thing' you were thinking about?"

He sighed. "Don't be so defensive. I just want to talk."

"No, thanks," Leanne scoffed. "I know how you *talk*."

During Leanne's first week on her dishwashing job, Brent had grabbed her in the kitchen, demanding that she go out with him. And more recently he'd harassed her at the amusement park down near the beach. Both times Brent had touched her as if she were something to be crumpled and tossed away.

Brent glanced up again. This time all the arrogance had disappeared from his face. "I'm serious," he said. "I'm sorry. I know I didn't treat you very well."

"Talk about an understatement."

"Okay!" He flicked hair out of his eyes. "But think about it from my point of view. I got moved to this town. I didn't want to come here. All of sudden I'm Brent Tucker of the Tucker Resort. People typecast me. It made me pretty angry for a while."

Leanne didn't react.

"Look, I'm not proud of how I treated you." He sighed. "You know, you weren't exactly Miss Nice-and-Polite to me, either."

"Tough luck," Leanne answered.

"It is tough luck." He stood up and tapped his racket against his thigh. "Okay, I acted like a jerk. How many times do I have to say it? I'm sorry. I feel like starting over. I want to change."

She scoffed.

"Come on, Leanne. What more can I do?"

Leanne fixed her gray eyes on him. She did see something new in his face, but she still didn't believe him. She didn't want to believe him because that would contradict everything she'd decided about the world — that she was alone, and everyone was against her. Sorry didn't help; luck was always tough, and people never changed. That had proven true in the past, and she saw no reason to let down her guard and learn those nasty lessons all over again.

She reached into the locker, pulled out her antique man's pajama top, slipped it on, and rolled up the sleeves. Pretending that Brent wasn't even there anymore, she walked up to the mirror and put on her usual heavy coat of red lipstick.

"That's all, I guess," he said as he started to shuffle toward the door. "I really just wanted to apologize. I know your life is hard, and I didn't mean to make it any harder."

She glanced at his reflection in the mirror, tried to focus on her own face again, but went back to looking at him. Despite the fact that he'd been cruel, she still wanted to stare at his beautiful, elegant face. With his head hanging down and his hair flopping over one eye, he suddenly looked boyish and sad. No wonder girls at school fell all over him.

Just before he reached for the door handle, she stopped him. "So what's different?" she asked. "What's changed?"

"Hm?"

"You said you've changed," she reminded him. "Or you wanted to change. Why?"

He thought for a minute. "Something happened to me this last weekend. Someone happened to me. I had an important weekend. With an important someone." He thought again and began to look very serious. "Very important."

Now *that*, Leanne believed. For a moment she was almost jealous of the someone Brent was thinking about. But that thought was wiped out by her awareness that something important had happened to her that past weekend, too.

Then, just as Leanne thought Brent was going to leave, he lunged toward her instead, and her heart began to pound. She backed against the locker doors.

But he merely held out his hand and offered an easy smile "Shake?" he asked. "Friends?"

Friends, Leanne thought. She considered the concept of "friends" about as inviting as crowds or niceness or luck. But he was her bosses' son, so she accepted his handshake, staring down at her milky skin next to his coppery tan. Brent grinned in triumph. He tightly grasped her fingers, then he nudged her with his shoulder before walking out the door.

When his footsteps faded away, Leanne found that she was shaking. She took deep breaths as she gathered her few belongings and stuffed them into her patchwork velvet bag. She suddenly felt the way she often felt at school. Get out. Get away. Get alone.

She took the side exit, which she considered good luck, then she cut through the parking lot, circling a few cars in a superstitious route. She zigzagged across the street until she was on the prom, the concrete walkway that ran along the beach.

For a moment she felt safe in the moonlight, listening to the waves as they rocked and rolled. She breathed in sea air. She hummed to herself and was actually singing out loud when she saw another boy perched on the retaining wall that protected the prom from big storms.

At first she thought it was Brent again, and

she wasn't sure whether to stop or run. Then she realized that it wasn't Brent at all. It was Chip Kohler, another Crescent Bay High junior. A totally different Crescent Bay High junior. Leanne couldn't believe that Chip was really waiting for her, so she kept a steady pace with her head down. Chip was the flip side of Brent. He was also blond, but unlike Brent's brilliant color of gold, Chip's hair was soft beige, like wheat or puppies. It was long, too. Longer than hers. He was much thinner than Brent. Taller, too. That night he wore a sweatshirt with some kind of recycling symbol, plus sandals, jeans, and a pair of glasses hanging from a cord around his neck.

He jumped down as soon as she strode by. "Wow. Hi."

She kept walking.

He cleared his throat and struggled to keep up. "I was just down on the beach. There was this whale-watching society meeting. Of course, no whales showed up. I guess they don't call to say, 'I'm not coming, hold the whale food.' " He laughed nervously. "Anyway, I remembered that you work at the resort and I thought I might run into you. Is that okay?"

"Is what okay?"

"For me to run into you? I don't want to bug you or anything. I just wanted to see if you needed a ride home. My van is parked up on fourth street."

It was weird. Brent barged in on her while she was dressing, while Chip acted like he should take a number just to offer her a ride home. Still, Leanne kept walking, past the aquarium and the hot-dog stand that was shaped like a giant clam.

"Leanne, do you remember me?" Chip finally asked, the sweetness in his voice turning a little sad.

She pretended not to remember, even though she would never forget. Chip was close to Jojo Hernandez, who was a Crescent Bay High popularity queen, a cheerleader for God's sake! Chip's crowd included Gabe Sachs and Kat McDonough, who ran a big deal radio show. And Miranda Jamison, who was a straight-A student and junior class president. Not one of them was Leanne's type, exactly. In fact, not even pathetically close.

But Chip was trying to be nice. She had to answer. "I remember," Leanne finally mumbled.

Chip was part of the important thing that had happened to her over the weekend. Chip had invited her to a party at Jojo's house, and she'd actually shown up. Of course, she spent the whole party on the front porch, where Chip had kept her company until he'd driven her home. Leanne remembered every moment of that ride in his noisy, beat-up van.

"Where do you live?" Chip had asked.

"Don't you know?" she'd dared. "I figured that everyone knew lots of things about me, even though most of it isn't true."

"I'm not too into gossip," Chip had responded. "Jojo told me you live on your own, though. That's cool. I mean, it must be tough, but it's cool. You don't have to talk about it if you don't want to."

After that, Chip had talked about stuff he was into — like the environment, sixties music, his classes, and his friends, of course. Leanne hadn't known what to say to that, so she'd sung along with the radio. A Lara O'Toole song had been playing. "Saturday's Girl." She hadn't intended for Chip to hear her, but he'd suddenly stopped the van and listened. Really listened.

"Whoa! You have a great voice," he said.

That had been important happening number two. Important happening number three came next, when he'd looked at her with such kindness and respect that she'd felt a little spark warm up inside her.

And now, standing at the intersection of Ocean and Third, Chip was gazing at her with that exact same expression.

"Anyway," he said. "I didn't mean to like jump out at you. My van is that way, if you want a ride. If you don't, that's okay, too."

"I don't need a ride," Leanne mumbled, unable to shake off her old defenses.

A tourist rammed into Chip. He quickly regained his balance with an embarrassed laugh. He took a deep breath, as if he were working hard to deflect her sourness. "Oh." He stuck his hands into his pockets, then blurted out, "You know I've been thinking about driving you home after Jojo's party, and that song you sang. I probably sound like a nerd, but I guess, like, I just want to say that if maybe we could get together sometime, that would be just great with me."

Leanne put her hands out in front of her, as if she were pushing something away.

Chip leaned toward her. "So, can we get together and just talk or something? You could

even sing for me again — I mean, if you wanted
to. I don't know the whole scoop on you, but
I'd like to find out."

Leanne looked up at him, seeing all the niceness that was missing from a guy like Brent
Tucker. She had a sudden impulse to sit down
right there, to take him up on his offer. She could
tell Chip her life story and sing him all her songs.

Instead she said, "Save it for the whales."

Chip gave her a confused stare. He wasn't sure
how he was supposed to react. She didn't know
how to react, either, so she darted across the
street. She was headed for her lucky route, down
the alley behind the bake shop.

Alone.

TWO

"WELCOME, SEA LIONS, TO THE CRES-
CENT BAY HIGH ANNUAL SPIRIT
DRIVE!"

The next morning Jojo Hernandez watched
from the bleachers as head cheerleader Brandy
Kurtz smiled for the huge crowd pouring into
the Crescent Bay High gym. Brandy's voice
echoed off the shiny floor as students climbed
bleachers and found folding chairs.

Jojo watched as Brandy stepped away from
the microphone and looked around for the rest
of her squad. Good, Brandy hadn't spotted her.

Normally Jojo would have been the first
cheerleader to grab her pompoms and race to the
gym floor. But since her party the previous
weekend, Jojo's five-hundred-watt smile had
burned out. Even though she was sitting on the
bleachers with her closest and oldest friends —
Kat and Miranda, Gabe and Chip — Jojo felt

paralyzed. She looked down at Brandy and watched.

"WE HAVE A TERRIFIC DRIVE COMING UP," Brandy announced to the crowd, when she turned to the microphone. "WE'RE GOING TO KICK OFF THE WHOLE THING TODAY. THEN WE'LL HAVE MORE RALLIES AND GAMES, PLUS THE SPIRIT DANCE. LET'S SHOW SOME SPIRIT!"

People stamped their feet and screamed. Everybody but Jojo. She looked like she should be in the mood. She, Kat, and Miranda had drawn identical waves across their foreheads in red "spirit paint," plus Jojo was in her cheerleading outfit, of course.

Even her pompoms were next to her on the bench. Still, Jojo couldn't get into the mood.

Brandy held up her hands, clearly enjoying her solo act before the crowd. "AND WE'LL END THE SPIRIT DRIVE WITH THE FAMOUS SPIRIT TALENT SHOW, WHERE YOU CAN ALL SHOW OFF YOUR SPECIAL SKILLS!"

Showing off her own special skills, Brandy did a high kick, followed by a stag leap. Jojo realized that she could linger a while longer in the stands. None of the other cheerleaders seemed to miss her. Brandy would be happy to hog the floor for as long as she could.

That was fine, because Jojo was more interested in Chip and Gabe, who were sitting to her right, while Kat and Miranda were together on the bleacher above. Chip was talking about Leanne Heard. Previously, Jojo had been addicted to gossip, but this was not about tacky curiosity, or the desire to find out information that she could trade or pass on. This was much deeper and more real.

"I don't think Leanne even remembered who I was last night," Chip was telling Gabe. He had his glasses on and seemed to be scouring the gym for Leanne.

Jojo looked around for Leanne, too, but couldn't find her.

"Maybe I shouldn't have surprised her after she got off work," Chip went on. "I waited for almost an hour, and then I only talked to her for like three minutes. She wouldn't let me drive her home. I don't want to bug her if she's not interested. Do you think she's not interested in me, Gabe?"

"Don't ask me, Chip," Gabe advised with a worried, but supportive, smile. "Ask Leanne."

"But you know about this kind of stuff. All I ever do is act like a nerd with girls. I talk to them once, and then I'm practically begging them to go out with me. I never give up until it's past hopeless. I keep asking myself, What would Gabe do?"

"Me?" Gabe laughed and shook his head. With his dark curls, tight black T-shirt, jeans, and radio dj voice, Gabe was usually the king of flirts. But since her party, Jojo had noticed that Gabe's flirting had become a little lackluster. He seemed different: more sober, more concerned.

"I just blabbed at Leanne like a moron," Chip went on. "Talk about wearing my heart on my sleeve. Gabe, you would have been cool and made Leanne laugh. You would have asked her to dance across Ocean Avenue in the moonlight or challenged her to play volleyball with one of your rolled-up socks."

"Chip," Gabe explained, "I don't think either of those techniques would have worked with Leanne Heard."

Chip shrugged. "Maybe you're right. I just want it to work out this time. I don't want Leanne to be another one of my weird crushes. I really like her. I want to get to know her better. She's different.

"You can say that again," Gabe sighed.

The boys both propped their chins on their fists as Jojo realized why she was stuck on Leanne Heard, too. It was because Leanne was the only part of her horrendous party that she could bear thinking about. Even after Jojo had tried to un-invite her, Leanne had still shown up at the party, which had taken a lot of nerve. Jojo suddenly admired acts that were courageous and gutsy.

Jojo didn't feel that she had shown guts at her party. First she'd been freaked out because she'd kissed Brent Tucker, who was Kat's big heart-throb. That had *not* been a courageous act. Jojo still hadn't found the nerve to tell Kat about it. And then, when Kat, Brent, and even Miranda hadn't shown up at her party, Jojo had gone into such a panic she'd locked herself in her room. When she'd finally gathered the courage to come out, she'd overheard Brandy and some other popular guests giggling about what an airhead, smile queen she was. *Smile queen*. Ugh! She'd hated hearing that. When the party was over, Jojo had vowed to be brave and undergo a change.

Miranda leaned down and tapped Jojo's shoulder. "Jo, aren't you supposed to go down and cheer?"

Jojo looked up at her two friends but didn't answer. Even with the dopey spirit wave drawn across her forehead, Miranda looked class-president smart and important. Her long, dark hair was fastened back in a French braid, and her lacy blouse was neatly tucked into her pleated skirt. Meanwhile Kat looked funny and original in walking shorts and paisley suspenders. She fingered that weird, twine necklace she always wore, which held a button advertising KHOT radio, a whistle, and a spirit drive schedule stuck on with a clothespin.

When Jojo still didn't respond, Miranda pulled her notebook out of her briefcase. "So when should we schedule the talent show meeting?" she asked Kat. "You and I had better do most of the planning on this, or it will never get done."

Kat nodded and tooted the whistle hanging around her neck. "We can have the planning meeting any time except lunch today. That's when Gabe and I have to face Vice Principal Hud about that graffiti in the cafeteria."

"You're kidding!" Miranda cried. "I didn't know Hud even knew about that awful graffiti."

"Of course he knows about it," Kat answered. "Attilla the Hud probably knows how many pieces of chewed gum are under every desk in this school."

Jojo knew about the graffiti, too, even though they weren't asking her opinion. The letters *KAT* had been scrawled in red paint on the brand-new cafeteria wall. Everyone knew about it, although no one knew if Kat McDonough was the Kat in question.

"I'll schedule the talent show meeting for Friday then," Miranda told Kat.

Kat nodded. "I'll tell everyone."

Miranda looked up from her notes. "Kat, you had nothing to do with that graffiti. Why do you and Gabe have to go in?"

"Because Hud called us in," Kat came back, still ignoring Jojo. "He probably thinks we did it to promote our radio show."

"Do you have any idea who did it?"

Jojo looked up, fixing her dark eyes on her friends.

Kat bit her lip, then gave Miranda one of their secret I'll-talk-to-you-later looks.

Jojo wanted to scream. Kat and Miranda left her out whenever they discussed something meaningful or important. Jojo wondered if it was better to be alone like Leanne, than to be snubbed by your very best friends.

As if she'd read Jojo's mind, Kat leaned over and rested her chin on Jojo's shoulder. "Jo, are you okay? You're so quiet."

Jojo stared straight ahead. "So. I'm quiet sometimes. What's wrong with that?"

Kat climbed down and sat next to her. "You're not quiet very often. And something is wrong. You've been really gloomy ever since your party."

Miranda leaned down, too, and tousled Jojo's hair. "Jo, you know we're both sorry we didn't come. I explained what happened with me."

Kat took a deep breath. In a softer voice, she said, "Jo, you're not upset about Brent Tucker, are you?"

"What?" Jojo gulped.

"Oh, Jo," Kat sighed. "I know you kissed him last week. It doesn't matter. I don't care."

"You don't?"

Kat threw up her hands. "Isn't that amazing? Me, the original come-out-of-retirement, go-nuts-over-a-guy-and-act-like-a-maniac, saying it doesn't matter if my friend kissed the guy I liked."

Jojo held her breath.

"But it's okay," Kat insisted. "Brent and I had a very weird time the night of your party. I

finally told him off. He and I are over. Done."
She pretended to draw a knife across her throat.
"Kaput."

Jojo was stunned. Kat knew that Jojo had
kissed Brent and didn't say anything about it for
a week! Kat told Brent off over the weekend and
was only admitting it just now, at the beginning
of a rally, as if she were reporting what the cafeteria was serving for lunch! Meanwhile, Jojo
had practically had a breakdown worrying that
she had backstabbed one of her best friends.

Jojo knew she had endured the last straw. Of
course, it was good that Kat wasn't upset and
that Brent wasn't some big thing between them.
But the way that Kat had told her — or not told
her — was just one more slap to Jojo. It was
final proof that Jojo was considered a shallow,
unimportant person.

Jojo wanted to go someplace where she could
be alone to think, but just then she noticed that
Brandy was flagging her from the gym floor.
All the other cheerleaders were lined up, and
Brandy was trying to hide her irritation behind
a forced smile.

"I'd better go."

Without saying good-bye, Jojo scrambled
down, barely noticing that she stepped on toes

and knocked her shin. Soon she was out on the floor with the other cheerleaders and at it again, smiling and kicking in unison. Still, the spirit paint, her cheerleading outfit, and the glitter that dotted her dark curls suddenly made Jojo feel like an Easter egg, a decorated shell without a center.

Jojo searched the bleachers for an answer. She saw Brent in the first row, surrounded by the senior BMOC crowd. But it wasn't until she finally spotted Leanne, who sat in the corner, completely alone, that Jojo realized that if she were going to change she would have to start right that second.

Jojo stopped in the middle of her routine, freezing as if she'd been turned to stone. A moment later, Brandy rammed into her, her shoes squeaking to a stop, her pompom flying into Jojo's face. Both of them tottered, then fell to the floor.

"JOJO!" Brandy shrieked as she scrambled up again.

Jojo didn't move. The spirit paint was making her skin feel brittle, as if her whole face might crack.

"JOJO!" Brandy repeated in a furious whisper. *"GET UP! What are you doing!"*

Jojo wasn't sure. All she knew was that she was about to find out.

Someone had written Kat's name in huge letters on the cafeteria wall, and what was she doing? Scribbling in a tiny barely legible hand, across a piece of notebook paper. *Brent, Brent, Brent, Brent, Brent, Brent.* A hundred, two hundred times, while waiting for Gabe on the floor outside Mr. Hud's office.

Kat had thought she was through with Brent. She'd used her head for once in her overly emotional, jokey life. The night of Jojo's party Brent had taken her to visit his old friends, only to get drunk and throw himself at another girl. She'd told him he was slime. She'd told him flat out she never wanted to see him again. And then she'd called Gabe, who'd come to pick her up.

Since Saturday, Kat hadn't seen Brent, except in passing when he was chatting with the cool older jocks or ignoring the stares from the prettiest girls. But she'd felt him, nonetheless. That's what she'd wanted to talk to Miranda about. Even though she had no idea if Brent had been connected to the graffiti stunt, she had to wonder. No. He hadn't. Had he?

As soon as Kat saw Gabe, the tension in her

stomach began to ease. Since Gabe had driven her home on Saturday night, she'd begun to appreciate everything about him.

"Oh, good," she sighed as Gabe jogged up, a Walkman clipped to his belt, the headphones hanging around his neck. "It's you."

Gabe did a little bow. "Brilliant observation."

"Don't get smug." She clutched her book bag, which was covered with plastic dinosaurs and trinkets. "I just meant, I'm glad you're not late. Hud the Dud is waiting for us."

Gabe pulled Kat to her feet. She popped up, and for a moment she had the oddest sense that he was going to pull her in and hug her. Not that a hug would have been all that weird between them. For the longest time she and Gabe had been like brother and sister, but lately something had changed. A while ago, an embrace had almost turned into something else, and since that time their relationship had gone up and down, forward, and backward. For a while they'd even stopped speaking and even canceled their KHOT show.

"Hi," he breathed. Her face was close to his.

"Hi," she said.

"Hi."

She blushed, punched his arm, and looked

around. "Come on, Gabe. I'm nervous about facing Hud."

"Why? Do you have a guilty conscience?" Gabe gave her a hard, jealous stare.

"Do you?" she tossed back.

"My conscience is always guilty."

Kat was happy to settle for a joke. She didn't want to bring up any suspicions about Brent. She didn't want Gabe to get jealous again, especially since she knew she wouldn't say anything to Hud. How could she say anything? She didn't know anything. Not really. Maybe the graffiti had been done by Kat Barthelme, a sophomore who was on the swim team with her.

Hoping to avoid the subject of Brent, she was relieved when Gabe swung into KHOT routine mode. He put on his Lounge Lizard character and leaned into her. "Come here often?" he leered.

Kat answered as Miss Grundy, her prim old lady character. "Actually, Hud the Stud and I have been an item for some time."

"Really? Does he give you unlimited hall passes?"

"Does he ever." Kat laughed. "Have you been here before?"

"Once. I mugged Mr. Hud in the hall."

Kat shook her head. "Gabe, you turkey."

Gabe was making a *gobble gobble* sound, when Mr. Hud stuck out his bald head and gestured for them to step in.

"Come with me," Hud ordered.

Gabe quickly stuck his Walkman into Kat's sack and they followed Hud into his nondescript office, sat down in the nondescript vinyl chairs, and then looked silently out the shaded window behind his desk. Unlike most of the campus, which smelled like the nearby ocean, Hud's office smelled of eraser shavings.

Mr. Hud cleared his throat and folded his hands. He stared straight at them with the expression kids referred to as "The Interrogator." "So do you two have any information about this cafeteria graffiti prank?"

Kat shook her head with a lame smile.

"I don't know anything, sir," Gabe said.

Mr. Hud looked skeptical. "We have a lot of activities coming up for spirit drive, and I want to make sure that this graffiti nonsense isn't the beginning of more trouble."

Kat shot Gabe a secret look with her mouth pursed and her eyebrows raised. Gabe stifled a smirk.

"You two are emceeing the talent show, right?" Hud made sure.

"Yes, sir," Gabe reacted, a little too fervently.

Kat didn't say anything. She was suddenly on the verge of giggles.

Mr. Hud glared. "I want to be proud of that talent show. If anything else happens, I will take it as a very serious offense."

"YES, SIR!" Kat and Gabe said at the same time. Then they met one another's eyes, and Kat knew they were lost. Her shoulders began to shake, while he couldn't wipe the grin off his face.

Hud stood up and pointed. "I'm glad you two think this is so funny."

Gabe took slow breaths.

Kat made little squeaks.

"I'll be watching you and your friends," Mr. Hud lectured. "You've always been good kids, but I don't like this new attitude. I'll be watching for any signs or signals of things getting out of control. I expect you to act responsibly."

Gabe stared at the floor. Kat was managing to look contrite.

Mr. Hud sighed. "All right, out of here. But remember, no more of this destructive fooling around."

By the time they were out of the door, Kat and Gabe were laughing again, groping for each other as they stumbled down the hall.

"As soon as he looked at me I knew I was going to lose it," Kat gasped.

"Me, too," Gabe agreed, slipping his arm around Kat's back. The giggles bubbled up again.

A teacher stuck her head out and shushed them.

"We'd better go to class," Gabe said, still stifling laughter.

"I have to go to my locker first."

"You want me to walk you?"

"To my locker?" Kat made a face. "Gabe, it's okay. I don't need any more rescuing, or escorting, or you stealing my lunch out of my locker so I won't have anything." She flexed a muscle, then kicked him sideways. "And you don't need to be any later to class. Go."

He wolf whistled as she took off. She didn't give him another thought until she'd jogged down half a hall and whipped open her locker. Then she gasped as what looked like a hundred little envelopes tumbled out.

Kat fell to her knees, trying to gather them,

and grateful that no one was there to see. "What is all this?"

Her breath on hold, Kat scrambled to pick up the envelopes. One by one, Kat tore them open. They were all valentines, even though it was eons until Valentine's Day. Each was different, but all had one word handwritten across them in fat red letters. *Love. Always. Forever. You. Forgive. Kat. Brent. Yes. Sorry. Me. Mine.*

Kat managed to shove all the envelopes back into her locker and wondered if she could crawl in with them. Hud was right; something here was out of control, and she didn't trust herself to act responsibly. Realizing that one larger envelope was still sitting on her locker floor, she reached for it and slowly opened the flap.

It was a lacy heart with a determined-looking cupid. Scrawled across, in Brent's elegant hand, was more than one word. It read: *You once told me to write your name on the school walls. Now I've done it. Give in, Kat. I won't give up.*

Kat's heart felt as if it had dropped through the floor. She looked up and down the hall, then slipped the note into her pocket. She wasn't sure whether to burn it, frame it, keep it forever, or hand it right over to Mr. Hud.

THREE

"Kat," Brent Tucker whispered, even though she was long gone. "Kat."

Brent wrapped his arms around himself and took a deep breath. The hallways were almost empty now. The tardy bell had rung. Brent didn't care. The only thing he really cared about anymore was seeing Kat McDonough and getting her to talk to him, but that was proving difficult.

He'd come close just before the bell. He had lingered near her locker but far enough away so that she wouldn't spot him and then rush off in a huff. There Brent had spied on her. He'd watched as she discovered the note he'd put in her locker. He'd seen the expression on her face as she reacted to what he had written.

Once Kat had almost seen him, but luckily

he'd stepped back just in time. After that she'd closed her locker, then hurried right by on her way to class. His note had been pressed against her heart.

Brent sighed. That was good. He was the new Brent these days. And the new Brent was careful. He didn't make impulsive moves. He took his time. He showed a little more self-control.

Brent scuffed his expensive loafers against the waxed floor. This wasn't going to be easy.

Still, he had his strategy planned. After Saturday night, he'd realized that he needed to change his approach. His plan now was to surprise Kat, to disarm her, then to get her alone and show her the new Brent. He'd tried the new Brent out on Leanne, and she'd bought it. She let down her guard, standing there in the dressing room as if they were intimate friends. She even shook his hand.

Brent had never had to work this hard for a girl, and he was actually enjoying it. That was because he'd underestimated Kat in the first place. When he'd first met her, he'd assumed she'd be putty in his hands — like every other girl he'd known. It was that way for a while, but only for a while. Then he made some wrong moves. Stupid moves. Kat had turned the tables on him. Amazing. No girl had ever done that to him before.

But no girl had ever made him feel this way.

Brent strode brazenly down the hall outside the main office. In his sharply creased trousers, suspenders, pin-striped shirt, and Rolex watch, he was in sharp contrast to the Crescent Bay High losers and small-town oafs. What's more, he wasn't wandering, or meandering, or just hanging out to wait and get in trouble. No, he was like an arrow that had reached high velocity and was going after his target, even if she'd temporarily slipped out of his view.

Brent was on a mission: gathering information. Since Saturday night, he'd hidden around the corner from Kat's house and spied. He'd found out her class schedule, so that he could be near the doorway to see her walk in and out. He knew her break, her study hall, and the route she took to the public swimming pool for her workout after school. And when he didn't know what she was up to, he watched closely so that he would find out. Like the trip she and Gabe had just taken to the vice principal's office — Brent had seen them go in, and he'd seen them come out. He'd watched them walk down the hallway together, all giggly and palsy, and then he had ducked out of sight to watch Kat's reaction when she'd opened her locker and read all his notes.

All his spying told him that Kat would take the bait. Soon. He would live, eat, breathe, drink *Kat, Kat, Kat,* until she forgave him. And she would forgive him. Kat was his — whether she knew it or not. His territory, his girl.

Suddenly Brent heard the *clack clack* of heavy wing tips slapping against the linoleum floor. Completely cool, Brent stepped right into the middle of the hall, while Mr. Hud marched up as if he were in a military parade.

"Hall pass!" Mr. Hud barked. He stuck out his hand.

"Of course." Brent pretended to reach into his notebook. Then he stopped and stuck out his hand, just the way he'd presented his handshake to Leanne. "I don't know if I've met you, sir. Principal Willis registered me when I first came with my parents. But I've been wanting to meet you."

Hud frowned.

Brent smiled his dimpled best. "I'm Brent Tucker."

Hud hesitated, then shook Brent's hand. He had a handshake that could crush rocks. "Tucker?" he questioned.

Brent hung his head. "I know. You probably hate my parents' new resort. You probably think we ruined that whole beach and that no one should develop that coastline at all."

Hud clearly didn't think that.

"My dad always says he's contributing to the town's economy." Brent gave an Aw-shucks-what-do-I-know?-I'm-just-a-kid shrug. "You should come by sometime and try a free dinner at the resort."

Hud's eyes began to sparkle. "Really?"

"Sure. I'll tell my dad. Bring your family." Brent forced himself not to smirk as he pictured the tank of a woman who probably had the misfortune to be Mrs. Hud.

"Thank you."

Brent nodded. "I'd better get to class. I have computer lit this period, and Mr. Melman asked me to pick up a piece of software from the library." He patted his pocket, careful not to harm the phantom floppy disk. "Nice to meet you, sir."

"Nice to meet you, Tucker," Mr. Hud called after him. "Welcome to Crescent Bay."

Brent turned back and waved. Then he took the long way back to his class, passing Kat's locker again so he could run his hand over the door as he strolled slowly by.

"Leaaaaaaaaaanne."

During the break before seventh period, Leanne moved fast.

"Leanne, it's spirit drive. You could as least smile."

Leanne averted her eyes.

"Why don't you talk to us, Leanne?"

She pretended not to hear.

"Oh, look. Leanne's ignoring us."

"Really? I'm soooo hurt."

"Maybe you should ask to borrow her lipstick."

"Leanne would never let you. She doesn't like us."

"Why not? What did we ever do to her?"

"Leanne doesn't need a reason not to like people.

"She's so weird."

Leanne had passed the girls gathered in front of the bathroom mirror, but she could still identify the voices and understand every nasty word. This time the comments had come from red-

headed senior sexpot Lisa Avery, and head
cheerleader Brandy Kurtz, who was in Leanne's
English class. But it didn't really matter who the
girls were. For Leanne, the insults came from
everywhere. Maybe she even asked for them.
By wearing high heels, red lipstick, and thrift-
store clothes, she certainly didn't dress to fade
into the scenery.

Leanne pushed through the crowd with her
shoulder. Get to the sink, skip the mirror, get
out, she told herself.

Whenever possible, she skipped the hall bath-
rooms altogether, and used the big, anonymous
gym bathroom instead. It was just like at lunch,
where she skirted off on her own to the secret
nook of the back staircase leading up to the music
room. But sometimes she was bound to get
caught in a crowd. Sometimes she had no choice
but to be in a place where other kids gathered
to socialize and gawk.

" 'Bye, Leanne."

"See you in class, Leannnnne."

"Call me sometime, Leanne."

"Hey, Leanne, who does your hair?"

Leanne finally made it out of the bathroom
and began her trek to English class. She blocked
out the memory of the voices, while a hundred

kids seemed to be pushing at her from all sides. She tried to keep her eyes straight ahead and not notice any of them in particular. Just like walking through a tunnel, she told herself.

As soon as she turned into the doorway to her English class, she halted to get her bearings. She noticed Jojo, who was already at her desk. Brandy appeared a moment later and pushed Leanne aside, storming over to use the pencil sharpener. From the nasty look that Brandy flashed Jojo, Leanne figured that Brandy was still annoyed about taking that tumble during the spirit rally. Actually, seeing Jojo and Brandy fall onto the gym floor had almost made up for the gossip and the nasty remarks. Like just about everybody else at Crescent Bay High, Leanne had been very entertained.

Leanne finally slipped into her own chair. Hernandez and Heard. Because of that weird alphabetical link, Leanne and Jojo sat next to each other in English and had lockers next-door, too. They couldn't have been more opposite. Jojo was so dark and taut and small. Her nails were decorated with red and white stripes, and her new clothes always matched. Meanwhile, dark roots were starting to peek out at the top of Leanne's hair. Her body was soft, ample, and everything about her was mismatched, from a single painted thumbnail, to the dress printed with Persian cats and worn with a rhinestone-studded cowboy belt.

"Hi, Leanne," Jojo whispered.

Leanne edged away from Jojo, as if just brushing elbows might give her permanent scars. Nonetheless, she stared at the line painted across Jojo's forehead. Leanne liked the spirit paint. It made her think of primitive art.

"Thanks for coming to my party last weekend," Jojo offered.

"Yeah, sure," Leanne mumbled. "I know you were thrilled that I came."

"I was glad. I really was," Jojo insisted. "I think Chip was glad you came, too."

Leanne brushed back wisps of limp, overdyed hair. She was waiting for the insult, the backhanded compliment. "Are you serious?"

"Sure," Jojo said in an almost shy voice. "I don't know if you even had a good time, but at least you came."

Leanne wasn't sure what Jojo was suddenly after, or why she was being so friendly, but she wanted to hear more about Chip. She didn't pursue it, however, because she didn't trust Jojo. And because Brandy, who was on the way back to her seat, had stopped in front of their desks.

Brandy's hair was brown with frosted streaks, so perfectly styled that she must have gone to the beauty parlor every other week. She played with her cheerleading charm as she glared down at them.

"Hey, Jojo," Brandy commented in a low, but nasty voice, "maybe if you stopped worrying about weirdos like Leanne, you might remember our cheerleading routines."

Leanne was ready to defend herself. A response was forming in her brain. But before it could reach her mouth, she saw Jojo lean forward.

"Hey, Brandy," Jojo snapped, "maybe if you stopped showing off so much, you might notice that pep assemblies aren't put on for your exclusive benefit."

Brandy's mouth fell open.

Even Jojo seemed stunned.

Leanne couldn't believe it. She felt as if an electric shock had just come up through her chair.

Just then the teacher ordered them all into a circle, so they could start their discussion of *Moby Dick*. As Leanne's desk scraped along the floor, her whole body echoed with what Jojo had just done. No one had ever stood up for her in the face of a powerful girl like Brandy! Leanne cast another glance at Jojo just to make sure she hadn't dreamed the incident, or read it in her book.

Jojo lifted her dark eyes and offered a smile.

Leanne still couldn't fathom it. Jojo was even more popular than Brandy. She's never seemed like someone willing to do anything that defied the majority opinion. Leanne wanted to say thanks. She wanted to talk about Chip, but as soon as class was over she hurried out, eyes down, cruising through that tunnel again.

FOUR

"ARE WE GOING TO GET THIS TALENT SHOW MEETING ORGANIZED?"

One hand cupped to her mouth, Miranda Jamison pleaded with her schoolmates. At least forty of them were packed into Mr. Bishop's drama room, which consisted of a small platform, black curtains, a hat rack hung with costume pieces, and a bare floor. People called it "the drama cave." Miranda never liked having meetings here. When kids didn't sit in chairs, it was chaos.

Miranda stuck her hands into her blazer pocket and stared down the entire room. People went on chattering anyway. Even Kat and Gabe, who were huddled together with Chip, were rehearsing a KHOT routine. Shelley Lara and David Ronkowski were holding up crepe paper, arguing over the theme for the spirit dance. Only Jojo was silent. She stood by herself in the very back, wearing such uncharacteristically dark colors that day that she almost faded into the curtains.

"Brandy and Lisa, can you be quiet?" Miranda asked pointedly. She glanced back at Jojo again. But she couldn't think about Jojo for long, because there were too many other curious and troubling people in the room.

Lisa Avery flipped back her red hair, then sprawled out on her side, tugging her Spandex dress. Lounging as if she were in her bedroom, she kept mouthing off to Brandy and the rest of her adoring crowd, all of whom listened with great interest. After every sentence of Lisa's, the rest of them stared at Miranda and smirked.

"I know it's TGIF, and we all can't wait for the weekend so we can go to the beach," Miranda projected. She pulled her clipboard and copies of the meeting agenda out of her briefcase. "I've done a lot of the talent show planning on my own, but I need to go over some details with you!"

Kat stood up and blew the whistle hanging from her necklace. People stuck their fingers in their ears, then finally started to settle down

. . . all except Lisa, Brandy, and their social clones.

Jabber, jabber. Point, point. They seemed to be making a big deal out of challenging Miranda's authority.

Miranda realized what was going on. This wasn't everyday drama cave mayhem. This was Miranda on the hot seat. She was leading her first big meeting since the Turnaround Formal, and Lisa, who'd always been jealous of her honors and accomplishments, wasn't going to make it easy. Thanks to Lisa — *and* Miranda's own behavior — the recent details of Miranda's personal life had been practically written across the Crescent Bay High blackboards.

"QUIET DOWN SO WE CAN GET STARTED!"

As she grew more tense and more frustrated, Miranda thought of just making an announcement. *Okay, let's get this out of the way. For anyone who doesn't know by now (and that would only be someone who'd just come back from a long illness or a tour of the Far East), I ran out on my longtime boyfriend, football captain Eric Geraci, at the Turnaround Formal. I know it was a horrible thing to do, but for me it was right.*

After that, my father grounded me, and I was kind

*of invisible around campus for a while. Yes, I know
that invisible was not a good state for the junior class
president, but it was pretty complicated. See, I didn't
just leave Eric; I rushed into the arms of Jackson
Magruder, editor of our school paper. My father didn't
approve. Sure, Jackson and I are pretty different. I
take charge. He takes chances. But don't worry. Now
that's over, too, and I'm back in control, ready to lead
my class again. If you want any more info just send
Lisa a questionnaire.*

When Lisa still wouldn't shut up, Chip got up
on his knees and shushed her. Lisa glared at him,
but she got the point. Finally she plopped back
against Brandy, her glossy mouth closed in a
resigned pout.

"Thank you," Miranda said to Chip. "Let's
get to work." She passed out copies of the
agenda, feeling grateful that she could just take
care of business. That would help get her mind
off Jackson. She was still so confused and tender
from the split, she had to sneak into the bathroom between classes to cry. No doubt about
it. The romance with Jackson was a big, painful
hole in her heart, but Miranda still needed to
show her schoolmates that she was on top of
things.

"And thank you all for coming to this meeting," she continued in a strong, clear voice. "You all know why we're here this afternoon — "

"Yeah," called out Sam Stein, drama class clown, "to goof around, just like we'll goof around at the talent show."

Miranda didn't let Sam throw her. "No, Sam. The talent show will not be about goofing around. Kat McDonough and Gabe Sachs, our hosts of KHOT radio, will emcee."

Kat stood up, then Gabe pulled her down, only to be pulled down himself after taking a corny bow.

"Not that they don't goof around," Miranda explained, "but they goof around so well, that you don't know it's goofing around."

"It's comedy," Gabe informed in the voice of Mitch Make-It-Up, one of his radio characters.

Everyone laughed.

"That's the point of the show," Miranda went on, picking up steam, "to show off the very best, the most professional talent here at Crescent Bay High. I'm sure you all remember the show last year, and we hope to make this year's show just as good."

Kat applauded.

Miranda smiled down at her. "We'll be clean-

ing up the auditorium on Monday after school.
Kat, Gabe, Chip, and Jojo already volunteered.
Anyone who's willing to help is welcome, too.
And then we'll be holding auditions next Thurs-
day. Mr. Bishop, Roslyn Griff, and I will judge
the auditions, just like Mr. Bishop, the junior
class president, and the student body president
judged last year. We'll be auditioning performers
in four categories, just like last year, too. Singing, dancing, skits, and musical instruments or
bands. Just remember to sign up early for an
audition time, because we want the very best."

"What about the people who don't fit into
categories?" a boy suddenly called out from the
back of the room.

Miranda froze, literally stunned by the sound
of his voice. He rose slowly, as if he'd suddenly
grown up out of the floor. He was wearing his
leather bomber jacket, a worn T-shirt, and army
surplus pants. His dark hair was a little spiky on
top, and a pencil was stuck behind his ear.

"Jackson," Miranda whispered.

She didn't know how she could have missed
seeing him, except that she'd missed so many
things about their relationship. She'd assumed
that she'd taken enough of a chance just by leav-

ing Eric and falling in love with Jackson Magruder. But Jackson had wanted her to go much further. He'd wanted her to face her father's disapproval first thing. Unlike Miranda, Jackson didn't believe in hiding or waiting while things got planned out.

Jackson put his hands on his hips. He fixed his green eyes on Miranda, then looked away as if the connection were painful for him, too. "I don't think our aim should be to try and make this show just like last year's. Let's not be so afraid of something new. Why don't we do something different for a change?"

"Like what?" Miranda managed. Her heart was pounding, and her legs felt shaky. She could sense everyone staring back and forth between her and Jackson. Lisa's eyes glittered with interest.

Jackson broke into his lopsided smile. "No offense," he said, turning his charm on the drama crew, "but if somebody does another dance to 'Puttin' on the Ritz,' or sings that song from *Cats* again, I'm going to go nuts."

"What's wrong with *Cats*?" Miranda looked to the drama people for support. But they were thoughtfully watching Jackson. Somehow Jackson had managed to practically tell them off without offending them. "What do you want to do instead?"

"What I'm saying is that we should really make this open to new things and new people," Jackson explained. "Let's not be afraid of a few surprises. What's the point of doing this if the same people are always in it, doing the exact same kinds of things?"

"What do you want, Jackson?" Miranda asked, starting to lose her temper. "Fireworks? Mud wrestling? Remember, it's a high school talent show!"

Jackson connected with her again, then he took a deep breath and turned back to the crowd. "Talent can mean a lot of different things," he explained with easy warmth. "I don't care if somebody shows off their pet snake or does a cooking demonstration, as long as it's interesting and even unexpected, then I'm all for it. What I'm not for is being such chickens that we rely on everything that's been done before and never have the nerve to find a better way."

Miranda knew that he was talking right to her, even though he was looking at the drama crowd, again. If only *she'd* had enough nerve, he meant. If only she'd been willing to buck her father's authority, to tell her dad that Jackson was important in her life. If she had been brave enough to do that, their relationship might have blossomed into something wonderful and new, instead of ending just when it had barely begun.

"What else do you think, Jackson?" she asked in a wary voice.

Jackson pulled out the little notebook he carried to jot down newspaper scoops. "I think that maybe some new people should be on the judging committee. That way some new and different people might feel like they'll have a real chance. What would you think of that? You three can still be on it, but let's get some other points of view, too."

"Like whose?" Miranda snapped. "Yours?"

"Anyone's," Jackson said. The crowd applauded. "Mine and about a dozen other people's from all different crowds. Let's listen to some different opinions for a change."

"How are we going to gather these different opinions?" Miranda argued. "We can't let everyone in this school be a judge. That would be chaos!"

"What's wrong with chaos?" Jackson shot right back.

Miranda felt Lisa's smug eyes on her again.

This was her big test, she realized. Would she
give Lisa justification to say, "Miranda Jamison
refused to work with Jackson. Her personal life
is getting in the way of her presidential duties"?
Lisa was giving her the same smarmy smile she
gave every time Miranda saw her in the halls,
hanging all over Eric, Miranda's ex.

And Miranda had more to worry about than
just Lisa. For all Miranda knew, her whole class
had been whispering behind her back. *Free Spirit
Jackson and Miss Perfect Miranda? Nooo. I bet every
time Jackson wanted to walk on the beach, Miranda
had to go home and study chemistry. She'd probably
have a nervous breakdown if she lost her 4.0. No
wonder the relationship only lasted a couple of weeks.*

Miranda wondered what they would all think
if they knew about the times she and Jackson *had*
walked on the beach. Actually, the walking
wasn't what Miranda remembered. What filled
her brain now were the memories of soft kisses,
or of running as fast as they could to each other
just so they could touch.

Miranda put her hand to her hot face and wondered if people could tell what she'd been thinking. She looked over her agenda again and tried
to get back on track. She still had to assign people to help clean the auditorium, work on

lights, usher, sew costumes, and sell program ads.

Lisa tried to start another round of applause for Jackson but he stopped it; he was obviously not thrilled to have her jump on his bandwagon. He went right back to Miranda. "It comes down to this. Are you so stuck in doing things a certain way that you're afraid to change?"

The room was silent. Everyone stared at Miranda. Even Jojo lifted her gloomy face with interest.

Miranda took a deep breath. She tried to push down all the chaotic feeling that was going on inside her. "Of course I'm not afraid," she finally said. Suddenly it was very important that she be even braver than Jackson. If he wanted to take one step, she'd take two. If he dared her to jump, she'd go ahead and try to fly.

"How about this," she said, holding up her agenda. "Let's throw this whole thing out and start over. How about if we have really open auditions? No sign-ups. Anyone who wants can just show up and try out. And they can do anything. No categories. And the judges represent lots of different groups at school, so there's no prejudice about who gets picked. Is that good enough for you?"

Jackson looked right at Miranda. "Now, *that's* my idea of a talent show."

Miranda glanced at Kat, then at Lisa, and finally back at Jojo, who was still standing alone looking thoughtful and dark. "We still need to vote on it."

Hands shot up supporting her new ideas. But Miranda knew that if she *was* really brave, she'd also admit the one big truth. She still loved Jackson. Everything he said got to her, and she would do anything to prove that she hadn't really let him down.

FIVE

"Gabe, don't you want suntan lotion?"

"Kat, I'm much too macho for lotion."

"Great, Gabe. I'll remind you of that when your skin is peeling off like a snake's."

"All right. If you insist. A little higher, Kat. Another inch to the left. Uh-oh, Kat. You missed a space."

"Gabe."

"While you're at it, Kat, could you peel me a grape?"

"Don't push it, Gabe."

That weekend, Chip sat on the beach, while Kat rubbed lotion onto Gabe's back, and the sun beat down on the five friends. Crescent Bay was still hot. The beach was crowded. Dogs barked. The sand glittered, and the waves were huge.

"You okay, Jo?" Chip asked as Kat and Gabe continued to banter and giggle. They all shared a huge army blanket. Miranda sat tall in a red swimsuit and matching cover-up, scribbling frantically on her clipboard. Gabe wore his sunglasses and classic black jeans cut off at the thigh, while Kat was in boxers and her swim team Speedo. Meanwhile Jojo had isolated herself on the one corner of the blanket. She sat pensively in a very un-Jojo-like old T-shirt with a blank diary open on her lap.

Chip was often the only guy who noticed when girls cut their hair or had a new dress on. It was obvious to him that Jojo was looking radically different all of a sudden. For the last two days, she hadn't worn makeup. Sure, they were just lounging on the beach, but Jojo usually would have been done up to the color of her toenails.

"You look different, Jo," Chip commented.

"Sometimes I think people put too much importance on appearances," Jojo said, then peered down into her book.

"I can't argue with that," Chip said, nodding. "You look nice, though. I mean, you looked nice before, but you look nice now, too."

Suddenly Jojo snapped her book closed and dropped it in the sand. "Chip, do you ever feel like everything in your life needs to change?"

"Me?"

Jojo looked right at him with confused, dark eyes. "You want to do something, and then you even *do* do something, but you're not sure it's the right something. And then you're not sure what to do next. All you know is that you have to do more. A lot more.

"Jojo, I'm confused," Chip admitted.

"Me, too," Jojo sighed.

Miranda suddenly scooted over to join them and nosed in. "Jo, if you want to really do something, make sure you show up on Monday to help the rest of us clean the auditorium." She put down her pencil. "And why don't you sell ads for the talent show program? We need help on the business end of things. I have a feeling we're going to have more kazoo players and fire-eaters than we can handle."

Jojo shifted sand through her fist. "Miranda, you weren't supposed to be listening. I was just talking to Chip."

"Believe it or not, Jo, I do listen," Miranda stated in a defensive tone. "I'm not so caught up in my own rules that I don't care what other people think."

"I know," Jojo insisted. "That's not what I meant."

Miranda reached back for her clipboard, then pulled out the pencil that had been holding her long hair in a bun. She jotted down more notes. "Okay, it's settled then. Simon Wheeldon will be your partner for selling program ads. He's in our class, and he's really high energy. You know him, don't you?"

Jojo looked at Chip, as if she weren't quite sure about this.

Simon was the head of the school's Young Entrepreneurs. Everyone called him Wheeler Dealer Wheeldon. He talked a little too fast for Chip, and wore saddle shoes and bow ties, but he *was* high energy.

"Simon was in our government class last year," Chip reminded. "Remember?"

"How could I forget?" Jojo grumbled. "He trades baseball cards and is always thinking up schemes to make money."

"You just have to sell ads with him," Miranda said. "Please, Jojo," she pleaded. "Suddenly this whole talent show thing has been turned upside down. It's making me crazy. I really need your help."

"Okay," Jojo sighed.

Miranda squeezed Jojo's arm. "Thanks."

Then she put down her clipboard and took off her shirt. She stared down at the crashing waves. "I have to stop thinking about this talent show for a few minutes. Anybody want to go for a swim?"

"Those waves are pretty big," Chip pointed out. "It's pretty wild out there today."

"I'm not afraid of wild," Miranda snapped.

"Okay," Chip said.

Miranda glared as another wave crashed down, then began marching toward the water.

"Come on, Chip. We'd better keep an eye on Miranda in case we have to play lifeguard," Gabe said as he jumped up and flexed his muscles. He reached down for Kat. "Kat, you come, too."

But Kat didn't budge. She stole Gabe's sunglasses and put them on. Then she stared up at the Tucker Resort, which hung over the cliff behind them like a jumble of glass squares. "I'll stay here. Some other people might come."

Gabe realized what Kat was looking at and flinched. Then he grabbed her and began to drag her toward the water.

"Gabe!"

"Come on," Gabe told her. "You're the swim champ, remember? You don't want to let your best friend drown." When Kat still fought him, Gabe picked her up and threw her over his tanned, bare back.

Now it was Chip's turn to stare at the Tucker Resort. The rectangles of glass glistened, and the outdoor elevator crawled up and down.

"Come on, Chip," Gabe called.

All day Chip had been trying to work up his nerve to walk up the beach and intercept Leanne a second, and possibly last, time. Even though he knew he was probably beating his head against a wall, he wasn't ready to give up. He wondered if he was just leading himself down another humiliating path. Chip Kohler, sixties-style hippie, nice guy, and total doormat. He shuddered.

Nonetheless, he told Kat and Gabe, "You two play lifeguard without me. I'm not a very good swimmer, anyway." He stood up and borrowed Jojo's brush to neaten his long hair. "I think I'll take a walk up the prom."

Gabe yelled at him in a knowing voice. "Up the prom?"

Chip put on his sandals.

"As in 'up the prom for a corn dog,' " Gabe pushed, "or 'up to the Tucker Resort to look for Leanne again'?"

Chip put on a dopey smile.

"Be careful," Gabe called out as Kat started to kick and scream into the water. "Jojo, don't let him fall for another weird girl!" A moment later, Kat had jumped down to tackle Gabe and throw him into the water.

"Leanne's not so weird," Chip whispered as he brushed sand off his baggy pants and his Earth Day anniversary T-shirt. He crouched back down to pick up his knapsack.

Jojo was chewing on her pencil.

"Do you think Leanne's weird, Jo?"

Jojo glanced up at the Tucker Resort, too. She shielded her eyes. "Not at all."

Chip tousled Jojo's curls. "Will you be okay if I leave you alone?"

"Everybody has to be alone sometime," Jojo decided. "It's good for me." She grabbed her book and opened it again.

Chip loped slowly up the beach, the sand slipping through his sandals with each stride. He was surprised to see Jojo acting so gloomy, but he wasn't really worried. Searching and thinking were good for people, he figured. All the philosophy books he read said you shouldn't be afraid of change, or pain, or seeing things in new ways. Besides, Jojo still hadn't quite gotten over crashing into Brandy at the spirit assembly. She'd sort of made a fool of herself, and Chip knew how that felt. He kicked at the sand and wondered — was he about to do it again?

Chip crossed the prom, then strolled across the Tucker Resort parking lot and through the lobby's revolving door. The lobby itself was quiet and filled with shopping mall air. Chip sat down on a sofa and waited. And waited. For almost an hour he read tourist brochures. Meanwhile he prayed that Leanne would walk by after her dishwashing shift. He drummed his fingers on an end table. He jiggled his knee. He kept waiting. He was endlessly patient . . . or endlessly pathetic, depending on how he looked at it.

"There she is," he blurted out. That was when he knew he was going for a second try, humiliating or not. Everything inside him felt lighter, as if his long limbs had been filled with helium. There was no turning back.

He'd caught a glimpse of Leanne winding through the parking lot. She must not have left through the lobby at all. She was walking fast. Chip got up from the seat in the lobby, went outside, and followed half a block behind. Leanne took odd and unexpected routes. She stepped into doorways, then went out again. She detoured up a few steps, down one, up again until she continued on her way. He lost her a few times. If it hadn't been for his faithful determination, and the unnatural sheen of the sun on her hair, he might not have tracked her.

He caught up with her at the corner of Ocean and Sixth. "Leanne?" He was out of breath but he lunged forward and tapped her shoulder.

Leanne spun around with a fierce look, as if he were a mugger. When she stared into his face she looked stunned, then suspicious.

"It's just me," Chip gasped. Even as the sidewalk crowd jostled him, he just stood and stared at her. Her gray eyes were filled with so many secrets. The expression in them seemed to fight him off and egg him on at the same time. If only they had some friend, or interest, or involvement at school in common, he might know which way to go.

Leanne began walking again. "You scared me," she said in her tough, almost hoarse voice. She always sounded like a rock singer who'd been belting her guts out. At least this time she sounded as if she remembered who he was.

"Sorry," he panted. "I mean, excuse me. I wasn't trying — "

"To what?" she asked, not slowing her pace.

"Nothing."

Leanne walked faster, up Ocean Avenue, past a taffy store and Captain Roger's Seafood Grotto. She seemed totally comfortable making her way through the weekend tourist crowd, much more at ease than she ever looked cruising the halls at school.

Meanwhile, Chip stumbled on curbs and stepped on the backs of people's shoes. He caught up with Leanne again. She lunged into Eighth Street, and the light suddenly changed. When she stopped, he crashed into her and his hands went right to her soft hips, guiding her away from the oncoming cars.

"Sorry," he gasped, pulling his hands away.

"For what?" She quickly turned her head, and her hair fluttered against his cheek.

"I'm . . . just . . . sorry," he repeated, as they stepped back up on the curb. Her face was only inches from his. His heart thumped.

"Why are you sorry?" she repeated.

"I'm . . ." He sounded like the wimp of the century! *I'm sorry. Oops. Pardon me.* He might as well have been a little old lady.

The light changed, and Leanne hesitated this time, as if she were waiting to see what he was going to do. Chip knew that he had to take a different tack. Being wimpy and apologetic was the story of his life — so was being ignored, dumped, and passed over. And Chip didn't want to be passed over this time. He wanted to get through.

Tourists walked around them, jostling and looking annoyed. Chip found himself wishing that Gabe had come along to give him advice. Until recently, Gabe had been a flirtation whiz — until things got heavy, and Gabe backed out. Chip, on the other hand, ached for heavy. He kept looking for that one special girl, but he never got far enough to show her the guy beneath the come-on lines.

Leanne turned away and wrapped her arms around herself. She flashed him one last curious look before stepping into the street again.

Instead of a come-on line, the only thing that occurred to Chip was an honest question. "Why do you take such a weird route?" he called, swooping after her and pulling her under the awning for the Flying Eagle kite store.

"What?" she breathed. She looked around, then finally stopped walking. She clutched her purse, which was made from patches of velvet.

"You walk four steps up and then three down

and up another two," Chip explained.

She looked embarrassed. Her pale skin turned very red. "That's me," she scoffed. She made a face, as if she were trying to scare him away. "Weird Leanne."

"Is it a good luck thing?"

"Don't you believe in luck?"

"I never really thought about it."

"That's probably because you have luck once in a while," she challenged. "When everything goes wrong all the time, luck is all you want."

"Wow." He was doing it! He was talking to her. Not because of any macho, devious plan. It was just coming to him, a fun conversation that was helping to loosen things up.

"Was that what you were doing when I drove you home from Jojo's party?" he jumped in, not wanting to lose the flow of the conversation. "You just sang parts of that Lara O'Toole song, then hummed parts, like it was some kind of puzzle. It was so cool. Do you only know half the words?"

She just stared at him.

"Tell me," he pleaded.

She thought for a moment, her gray eyes still filled with suspicion. "Okay. It *was* just for luck.

Because I know that song better than I know my name."

"Anyway, it was nice." Nice . . . what a dumb word.

She rolled her eyes and started walking again.

"Can I tell you the truth about something, too?" he asked.

She didn't answer.

Here I go, Chip thought, diving in and probably breaking my neck. "I like you. I want to get to know you better. I want to share something with you, to find out what you're really like. How . . . or like, why . . . you know . . . under what circumstances would you want to go out with me?" God. If Gabe heard him, he'd die.

Leanne stopped and looked at him as if he was crazy. "Are you serious?"

"Unfortunately I am," he admitted.

She shook her head, shifting in her high heels and taking a deep breath. Finally she looked at him again. "Okay. Get tickets for the Lara O'Toole concert that's coming up. I'd give anything to go to that."

Chip remembered that Lara O'Toole was giving a concert at a club in Crescent Bay because the guy who owned it was an old friend. But there were only two shows. The tickets had been snatched up weeks ago. "That's impossible," he said.

"I know. Life is impossible," Leanne stated in a steely voice. "And getting to know each other better is probably impossible, too." She bolted across the street, wobbling a little and not looking back.

Chip knew that this was it. Either he made a bold move or he'd have poured his guts out again, only to be left in the lurch. He ran after her, catching her in front of the bookstore. They both stared in the window and caught their breath. "If I really could get tickets — not that I can — but if I could, then would you do something just as amazing?"

"What?"

He decided to just jump in and go for it. If she never did anything at school, he didn't know how they'd ever find a common ground. "Try out for the talent show at school."

She stood there as silently as if he'd just sentenced her to death. "No way," she finally said.

"But you only have to do it if I get those tickets," he said. "And you just admitted that's impossible. So why not make the deal?"

She turned to face him and stared into his eyes as if she expected him to laugh at her and walk away. And when he only looked back, treasuring the sight of her sad, smart eyes and dark red mouth, she finally muttered, "You're sick."

"No, I'm not," he wooed.

"Oh, all right," she finally grumbled, as if she were just trying to get him to leave her alone. "It *is* impossible. So why not make the deal."

"Great."

"It's not great," she mumbled. "It's not anything. It's just impossible." Then, without a smile and good-bye, or even another look, she darted off.

Chip stood on the sidewalk for a long time. He knew that he would never get those tickets and that she would never try out. Nonetheless, he felt that old Chip hope. Impossible appealed to him. Maybe that was even what appealed to him about Leanne.

SIX

Kat arrived at the school auditorium first. The Monday hall traffic had cleared, and the auditorium was waiting to be spiffed up and cleaned. The lights were off. Stepping inside, she felt for the switch. She reached, patted the wall, but she couldn't find it.

"Yoo-hooooo?" she called in her Patty Prom Queen radio voice. For a moment she thought she heard something, and her stomach flipped over. She looked into the big, dark space and she thought about Brent.

Stop. You are over him, she reminded herself. He's scum. Slime. A form of life that even Chip wouldn't recycle.

She took a step in. Do not go back. Do not return to go. Do not collect two hundred valentines, or five hundred flowers, or skywriting your name across the bay, or whatever he's going to come up with next.

Having finally made herself laugh, Kat walked all the way in, hoping to find the light switch on the other side of the room. Since the notes in her locker, Brent had left roses at her front door and classical music tapes on her homeroom desk. But she still hadn't seen him again face-to-face. And for some reason, that was only making her think and wonder about him more and more.

Groping her way in the dark, Kat smelled dust and old cloth seats. There was the constant hum of some kind of fan.

"Yow."

Kat's foot suddenly rammed into something. She lurched. It was just a box. A book. Maybe a piece of wood. She was still trying to figure out what she'd bumped into when she heard the auditorium door open and close again behind her. Swift, purposeful footsteps followed, and Kat's heart picked up. She spun around, still unable to see. The next thing she knew, someone had wrapped her in his arms and was nuzzling the side of her neck.

"Ohh," she breathed, feeling so warm that she thought she might faint. Against all better judgment, she turned toward him and leaned in, breathing warm skin and feathery hair.

"Want to dance?" he teased.

She was confused and dizzy. "Wait, please."

"What?"

"I don't know . . ."

"You don't?"

"Please . . . stop . . . I don't think . . ."

"Okay."

"I told you before . . ." she managed in an urgent voice. "No . . ."

"Kat, I'm just goofing around. Don't get all upset."

Kat's stomach felt like it was upside down. Her blood was pounding, and she couldn't think. Out of some strange reflex, she lifted her fists and flailed, until she became aware that she was touching a very familiar body, warm, worn cotton and soft, curly hair. She clung for a split second, then stepped back and caught her breath.

"All right, all right," he said in a humorous voice. "I didn't know you were so jumpy. I'll never try and sneak up on you again." Then he switched into his lounge lizard voice. "Or maybe I will. Come to think of it, that was kind of nice."

"Gabe!"

"That's my name."

Her pulse was still racing. "It's you."

"Who were you expecting? Count Dracula?"

"It's dark." Kat took deep breaths. Her hands were shaking. "What are you doing sneaking around in the dark?"

"I'll turn the lights on." Gabe patted her and quickly went back over to the door. "It's usually easier to clean a place when you can see. And since no one else volunteered to do this dirty job, Miranda's faithful cleaning slaves had better get to work." He flicked a switch and the first bank of lights came on.

Kat saw that Gabe's cheeks were pink. He was giving her a funny, embarrassed look. She collapsed onto a seat.

Gabe turned on the rest of the lights, then opened the door again and stuck his head out. "Oh. It looks like we're all here now," he said, ushering in Chip and Miranda who were armed with buckets and brooms. A moment later, Jojo straggled in, too, dressed all in black.

"You do remember these people, don't you Kat?" Gabe teased. "Of course, Jojo's looking a little different these days, but I figure you and Miranda have talked on the phone for about two million hours."

"Gabe, what are you babbling about?" Miranda asked as she strode by him and put her things on the stage.

"Nothing. As usual," Kat answered. She rubbed her eyes. Gabe was still staring at her, but her pulse was returning to normal. "Hi, everybody."

Chip held up his fingers in a peace symbol. Jojo gave a gloomy shrug.

"Yo, Chipper," said Gabe. He and Chip did an elaborate handshake, then helped one another onto the stage.

"Okay," Miranda said, taking the lead right away. She took off her blazer and pulled her clipboard out of her briefcase. "We need to move the piano, clean the trash, sweep, and sort through that storage area under the stage. Mr. Bishop wants us to see what's down there in case we want to use some things for the talent show."

Jojo flopped down into the seat next to Kat. "Miranda, I still can't believe you are making me do this," she moped. "It's bad enough that I have to meet Simon Wheeler Dealer Wheeldon downtown in a half hour." She picked the last bits of glitter off her nails. "I really don't think this is what I need to be doing. Isn't there something more important I could do?"

"Selling ads for the program is important," Miranda argued. "And I'm not *making* you do anything, Jo. I'm not a dictator."

"I know," Jojo sighed.

They went to work. Right away Chip took on the toughest job, pushing the old two-ton piano out of the wings. A second later Gabe skirted over to help him, while Miranda shook out a broom and Jojo picked up trash in front of the first row.

Kat flexed a muscle, then joined Gabe and Chip, even though they were managing without her. Gabe stared at her again, still trying to figure why she had overreacted to him in the dark. Maybe he had overreacted, too. At least his body sure had. His pulse was still racing, and his heart was still on overkill. What exactly was going on?

"I need your advice about Leanne, man," Chip told Gabe, as he went back for the piano bench.

Gabe didn't know if he had any worthwhile advice to give anymore. He'd always been the king of flirts and had even felt superior to Chip, who'd been the crown prince of rejection. But Gabe wasn't so sure of things anymore. Recently he'd flirted with a great girl at school, then felt like a fake when she'd wanted more and he hadn't been able to come through. He glanced at Kat and wondered if he was ready to take things more seriously.

"I know you think she's just another one of my weird crushes," Chip said, "but I swear, Leanne's different."

"I'll say she's different," Gabe tossed back. He didn't really know what else to say.

Chip brushed his long hair away from his eyes, then took in the girls. "I keep thinking that if only I could get her involved in stuff with us, things could work out."

"How are you going to get Leanne involved?" Gabe asked. "From what I can tell, she hasn't exactly been begging to join the Pep Club."

Chip sat down at the piano. He slipped his glasses on and banged out a few chords. "I sort of made this deal with her."

"What kind of deal?" Jojo piped up.

"You know that Lara O'Toole concert coming up at the Blue Cove Music Club? Leanne really wants to go. If I could get tickets — which I can't because the concert it sold out — Leanne might trust me more and not feel so hostile." He shook his head. "Forget it. I'm dreaming. It's impossible."

Gabe leaned on the piano. "Beware of trying too hard," he warned, even though part of him envied Chip's way of jumping into things. No matter how many bizarre girls Chip had fallen for, he still acted like Leanne was going to be his Cinderella. Meanwhile, Gabe had flirted with scores of eager girls and had tons of success. But he'd never gone beyond the flirting stage. From the minute he met a girl, he was already looking for a way to back out.

Jojo threw her trash into the basket. "Speaking of trying too hard, I have to go meet Simon. From what I've heard, he tries to bargain when he buys a candy bar at a football game." She gave Miranda a dirty look. "I can hardly wait." Then she left, slamming the door behind her.

"She's getting even weirder than Leanne," Gabe decided after Jojo was gone.

Kat shrugged. "Join the club."

Miranda hiked herself up on the edge of the stage and checked her clipboard. "Okay. Who wants to look through the costume storage? Kat, you know this place from drama class. Why don't you go down there?"

"Okay," Kat said. She smiled at Gabe. "You want to come with me?" She reached onto the stage and untied his high-top.

Gabe felt his pulse speed up again. The storage room was dark and secluded. "Into that dark place?" he teased. "Kat. I didn't know you cared."

"Okay, okay. Never mind," Kat decided, stopping him. "I just wanted somebody to move the heavy boxes."

"I'll go," he volunteered.

"Never mind!" Kat insisted. "I'll go by myself. I love heavy boxes. And dark, dusty places full of gorilla masks and old shoes."

Gabe smiled at her. "I knew there was a reason I picked you for my radio partner."

"You didn't pick me, Gabe," Kat called back to him. She headed slowly toward the dressing rooms, around the other side of the stage. "I picked you."

Gabe savored her words for a few minutes after she disappeared. Since Brent Tucker had — hopefully — dropped out of the picture, Gabe was beginning to get new vibes from Kat. At least he thought he was. Hmm. It was so hard to tell. But if something really did change with Kat, who knew, maybe he was ready.

The costume storage was underneath the stage floor, reached by a hobbit-sized door. Kat had been down there once before to find her costume for last year's production of *Fame* but she didn't have fond memories of the place. The ceiling was so low that she'd bruised her head, and the dust had given her a major allergy attack.

Sure enough, as soon as she ducked through the door, she sneezed. A low, flat expanse of shadowy boxes and racks stretched out before her. She could hear her friends' footsteps over her head and the faint *plunk, plunk* of Chip at the piano. At least she found the light right away. A bare bulb was hanging in the middle of the room.

She pulled the string and grumbled, "Talk about gross."

There were racks of moth-eaten clothes, cartons of hats, boxes of purses and gloves, and broken dime-store jewelry. Kat picked up a pair of fur earmuffs and put them on.

"AAH-CHOOO!"

She sneezed again, so violently that her neck hurt and her earmuffs flew off. Then she rubbed her eyes, which were really starting to water. Actually, her whole body felt as if it was under water. She still didn't know how she could have confused Brent with Gabe, or how she could have the same kind of feelings for two such different guys! Especially since one guy was sup-

posed to be like her brother/best friend, while
the other should have been a slimy person of the
past.

Kat was still trying to figure it out, when she
realized that someone else had slipped into the
storage room after her.

"Hi, Gabe," she whispered without looking
up. Her pulse sped up again. She told herself that
if it wasn't Gabe, it was just an illusion. A suit
of clothes hanging on the wall, or the stuffed
scarecrow left over from *The Wizard of Oz*.

"Kat," he said, in a clear, elegant voice.

Kat's stomach dropped through the floor.

"Hear me out, Kat. I want to talk to you."

Kat focused her watery eyes and saw Brent
Tucker blocking the door, his graceful body in
pleated trousers and a polo shirt with an argyle
vest and deck shoes. Even after everything that
had gone wrong between them, Kat was still
struck by the angular beauty of his face. Her
heart was pounding so hard she thought it would
knock her over.

"Hi," she said, trying to sound casual. The
last time she'd been alone with him, she'd told
him off with confidence and style. Why was she
suddenly so trembly? Was it only the grafitti?
The notes? The memory of him taking her to a

wild party, then ditching her to get drunk and flirt with other girls?

Kat grabbed a box of shoes, as if that would protect her from ever falling for him again.

Brent didn't move. He didn't even extend a hand or change the expression on his lean, beautiful face. It reminded Kat of the first time she'd met him outside the radio station. He'd just stood there, taking her in, as if *she* were the new student and he owned the school.

"I saw you and your friends go in here and I just had to follow you," Brent said. "I know I blew it with you. I know I treated you badly."

"You did," Kat managed.

"I'm messed up, Kat," he said, shaking his head. "If you knew my parents, you'd understand. I don't know how to treat a girl like you. I want you to teach me. You're the one who could make a difference in my life." He lifted his face and gazed at her.

Kat stared into his blue eyes, bluer than deep water. Her knees were starting to go weak. Brent held out his hand to her, and she found herself reaching out, too. She touched his fingertips, then drew back when he stepped in for more.

She prayed that Gabe would suddenly burst

in on them. She wanted Brent out of her life
. . . confusing feelings or not! Sometimes she
wanted to take *all* her feelings and plop them
onto Gabe. Lately Gabe felt so safe. Not just
safe, but right. Lately she even had these urges
of wanting more than friendship with Gabe, but
maybe that was just connected to her fear about
Brent — her real fear that she might fall for
Brent again.

"I've never felt this way about a girl before,"
Brent said with a scary intensity. "I'll do any-
thing to make it happen for you and me, Kat.
This time, it's no game."

Kat had the eerie sense that he was telling the
truth for possibly the first time. He'd given her
plenty of lies and excuses before, but there had
always been a smugness behind his dimpled
smile. Now she saw a determination that not
only scared her, but made her wonder what he
was going to do next.

"What do you want?" she asked.

"Just give me one last chance. Meet me alone.
Meet me somewhere without your friends."

The one thing Kat could never do again was
be alone with him. If she was alone with him
again, she'd be sunk. "No. I don't want to meet
you alone."

His eyes turned hard. He took a few steps toward her and held out his hand again. This time he didn't seem to be interested in a faint touch, but in something much more forceful and threatening. But he stopped himself before touching her. "You will meet me, Kat," he threatened. "If you don't, I'll find you."

"How about at the spirit dance, then?" Kat blurted out, praying that he would be pacified with meeting her in a public place.

He was clearly disappointed, but he finally shrugged. "All right. If that's the way it has to be. Meet me there." His golden hair glimmered even in the dusty light. "Just promise me one slow dance and give me one last chance to show you how I've changed."

Kat didn't want to promise him anything. But just being near him again was cracking open something inside her.

"I'll see you there." Brent reached out to her again with both hands, but he didn't try to make contact. He just caressed the air around her, as if actually touching her would be too dangerous. Then he whispered, "I love you." A moment later he was gone.

His final three words hung in the musty air for a very long time. As she stood in the dusty room, waiting for the image of Brent to fade away, Kat prayed for Gabe to come down and find her. When he didn't, she raced back up to the stage and threw herself at him in something halfway between a tackle and an embrace.

"Whoa," Gabe said, when they finally separated. "What's going on? Was there a bogeyman down there?"

Kat didn't answer. She couldn't, because she really didn't know.

SEVEN

Simon Wheeler Dealer Wheeldon drove one of the grossest cars that Jojo had ever seen. An old Chevrolet Impala with rusty fenders, torn seats, and a radio that hung halfway out of the dashboard.

"Sorry about the Wheeldon wheels," he said cheerfully, as they sped away from campus and down to Foster's Pizza. He leaned back, twirling the steering wheel with one finger. "It's all I can afford right now. You see, I don't have to worry about insurance in a wreck like this. But I'm saving up to buy something better. A Porsche. That'll be my next car for sure."

"I'd like to see that," Jojo said. Thinking of Simon driving a Porsche was like imagining Brent Tucker on a tractor.

"I guess I'm just trying to impress you," Simon chattered. There was a twinkle in his eye, and his short, red hair was curly in front, like a spring that had descended over his forehead. He wore a bow tie, and jeans that were so new they practically crunched. "I know you hang out with Miranda and the important crowd. And I know how you cheerleader types are."

"I'm not important, and I'm not a type!" Jojo insisted. She faced the window. "And you don't have to impress me."

"Impressions are important," Simon went on. "I know. It's like when we go in and sell these ads. Now we have to sell enough ads to pay for printing the talent show program. Right? But the people buying the ads will want to make sure that the ad they buy will improve their business."

Jojo rolled her eyes. "So?"

Simon took a fast corner without missing a beat. "So, people are going to size us up the minute we walk in their doors. If they think we're the type of kids who can't afford their pizzas or their track shoes or whatever they sell, they won't buy one of our ads. It's about what I can do for you, what you can do for me. That's it — trading and selling; first impressions and deals. Which is why I'll park where no one can see us. I don't want them to get a bad first impression from my car."

Jojo slumped down. "I'm just surprised you don't have a car phone." She didn't know what else to say. Simon was talk, talk , talk. He never stopped. He talked to her; he talked to the radio. He talked to himself if no one else would listen. He waved to passersby as they drove across Holiday Street. He was about as far from the answer to her problem as it was possible to be. Since standing up to Brandy Kurtz and defending Leanne, Jojo had been waiting for ner next opportunity to do something important or brave. Now she was stuck with Simon, and Simon could only think about wheels and deals. She could only hope that their afternoon together would be brief.

"Do you know those people you're waving at?" she asked as they pulled into the pizza parlor's parking lot.

"No, but I'm networking." Simon smiled and kept waving. "You never know when you'll need a new contact."

"Contact?" Jojo repeated. They parked next to the pizza delivery van. Jojo gathered her ad paperwork, while Simon checked his hair in the mirror. "Is contact a dirty word for friend?"

"Not at all," Simon said, craning his neck to examine his shave. "Sometimes it just means somebody who can help you out; do something for you; make a sale for you . . . a trade or a deal."

Jojo cringed.

"You don't have to be a snob about it. You didn't get on the cheerleading squad by ignoring people. You traded smiles for votes. I'm just honest about it."

Jojo still couldn't believe that in the midst of a major life crisis, she had been stuck with someone like Simon. She wondered how she would survive until she met her mother in front of the shoe store on Main Street. "Why does everyone have to be some kind of type?" she asked Simon. "Am I wearing my cheerleading uniform?"

He glanced at her.

Jojo had actually taken a cue from Leanne and bought a thrift-store skirt, which she'd put together with an old golf sweater of her father's. She'd let her hair go any which way and wore only red lipstick. She *was* still wearing her megaphone cheerleading necklace, but it was tucked inside her clothes. But somehow, even though she'd changed everything on her outside, she still felt the same.

Simon wrinkled his nose. "Hey, you look different than you used to look on the football field. Is that a costume for the talent show or something?"

"No."

"Nothing personal, but since you're dressing that way," Simon went on, "I guess you'd better let me sell the ads for the talent show program. They might think you're one of the homeless." He smiled and climbed out of the car.

Jojo folded her arms and refused to budge. She wondered if she deserved this afternoon with Simon, if it was the price she had to pay for her years of easy popularity. "I don't think that's funny," she told him.

It took Simon a moment to realize that she wasn't getting out. He leaned in. "What's the matter? Did I say something wrong?"

"I don't think jokes about homeless people are very sensitive," Jojo stated.

"Oh." He thought about it for a moment. "I guess you're right. Sorry."

Jojo still didn't get out of the car. "Let me tell you something," she lectured proudly. "I happen to have a friend — not a contact — who doesn't live at home. Maybe she's not actually on the street, but she had to move away from her mother because she was having a hard time! Now she supports herself and lives on her own."

Simon's face softened. His freckles seemed to fade as his skin grew red. "I said I was sorry. That's awful, though."

"Maybe it isn't so awful," Jojo argued. She was trying to figure it out. Sometimes she felt horribly sorry for Leanne and wondered what she could do to help, while other times she wished she could be Leanne and really experience the world, for a change. Hmm. Maybe that was the answer. Maybe if she tried life from Leanne's point of view, she'd do that important thing that she was striving for. "Maybe my friend is lucky," Jojo finally said.

"Lucky?" Simon screwed up his face.

Jojo nodded. "She's had to face a lot of hardship, so she knows about more things in life than just cheerleading. And she's certainly deeper than someone like you who just worries about contacts and sales. I envy her."

"You do?" Simon slipped on a jacket and re-adjusted his shoulders. "I don't. Hey, I'm sorry if I made an insensitive joke. But you don't

have to act so snobby. I was just talking. I talk
a lot."

Jojo sighed and thought of all the times she'd
just talked. In the past, chatter had been like food
to her, and thoughtless gossip was merely dessert. She wondered if she were doing the same
thing again, boasting about her "friend" Leanne.
For all she knew, Leanne wouldn't even admit
to knowing her.

"Never mind," Jojo said. "Let's go in. Miranda expects us to sell some ads for this program. We'd better get started."

Simon nodded and pulled himself together,
sticking his papers under his arm and a pen in
his pocket. Jojo slammed the car door and shuffled behind him.

The pizza parlor was hot; it smelled like rising
dough. A player piano was tinkling away near
the entrance, the keys moving eerily, as if a ghost
were sitting on the bench. As they waited to talk
to the manager, Jojo almost pretended that she
was Leanne for that moment. She imagined
being completely on her own. Independent. No
one to answer to. No one knowing what she
was really about. People would gossip about her,
but she really didn't care. She'd support herself,
sweat and slave over dishes in a restaurant

kitchen, then spend late nights writing poetry and reading books.

The pizza manager appeared, a guy who looked about nineteen and had a mustache and dingy blond hair.

"Hey, Simon," the manager said, slapping palms with Simon and doing a ridiculous handshake.

Simon laughed and laughed. "Hey, Mark. How's it going?"

"Got some new baseball cards to sell me?" Mark asked. "My collection's looking pretty good."

Simon shook his head. "This time it's ads in the Crescent Bay High talent show program. Every kid in school will see the show. That could sell a lot of slices. Don't you think so, Jojo?"

Jojo turned her back on him. This seemed even more pointless than waving her pompoms and kissing up to Brandy Kurtz. If it hadn't been for her loyalty to Miranda, Jojo would have walked off then and there.

Simon waited for Jojo to say something, then turned back to Mark. "Anyway, it's twenty dollars for a quarter page ad. I'll buy a large pizza myself this weekend if you take out an ad. What do you say?"

"I'll go check with the owner," Mark said. "I'll be right back." He brushed off his apron and disappeared.

"Gee, Jojo. You're a big help," Simon whispered while they waited for Mark to return.

"Sorry," she told him. "It's sort of embarrassing, trying to bribe a guy just to buy an ad."

Simon started to object, then relaxed when Mark returned with a crisp twenty-dollar bill.

"So what else are you selling this month, Simon?" Mark asked in a softer voice. He leaned over the counter. "You got any more of those college T-shirts from USF?"

"Not this month," Simon said.

"How about concert tickets? My girlfriend really wants to see The Spark when they play at the Dome."

Simon wrote out a receipt, then practically pole-vaulted over the counter to pat Mark's back. "I can usually get tickets — but you'll have to pay through the nose. I'll look into those Dome tickets and let you know. Thanks."

Concert tickets? Jojo perked up as they wandered back out of the parlor and into the sunny parking lot. If she really wanted to help Leanne, the best way might be to get Leanne together with Chip. And according to Chip, that hinged on getting Lara O'Toole tickets. For the first time in days, Jojo put on her old five-hundred-watt smile. Maybe *this* was the important thing she needed to do. "You can get concert tickets?" she asked Simon as they headed back to the car.

"Sure," Simon grumbled. He obviously felt that she'd insulted him. "Tickets for sold-out shows. Rare concerts. Even backstage passes sometimes. You name it."

She stopped and leaned on his heap of a car. "Can you get two tickets for Lara O'Toole this Friday night?"

"For you?" Simon asked. "Lara O'Toole's not exactly a cheerleader-type singer."

"The tickets are for my friend," Jojo admitted. "The one I told you about."

Simon thought for a moment, then straightened his bow tie. "I can get them. But it'll cost a hundred bucks. You get me the money tomorrow, and I'll have tickets for you the next day."

Jojo didn't flinch. She knew her mother would spring for it. "It's a deal," she said, reaching her hand over the car hood to shake. "I think I'm speaking your language."

Simon refused to shake. "Wait a minute. This

friend of yours barely has a place to live and you're going to spend a hundred bucks on two concert tickets for her?"

Jojo didn't have an answer for that. She thought about it as Simon sunk down into his car and gunned the engine. He almost took off before Jojo had a chance to slide in, too.

"You'd better drop me off downtown now," Jojo said as they pulled back onto Holiday Street. "My mom's waiting for me."

"But we've only sold one ad," Simon complained. "If we don't sell more today, we'll have to meet again next week."

Jojo knew she was letting Simon down, but she could only think about so many things at once. She couldn't wait to get home to call Chip. She was already wondering if it might be possible to get Leanne into their group, or for her to leave the crowd and just hang out with Leanne. All she knew was that she had her first surge of pride since telling off Brandy Kurtz.

Even before Simon slowed down on Main Street and Ocean, Jojo spotted her mother waiting in front of Baylor's Shoes. Her mom sat happily in her new Cadillac, reading a magazine.

When they slowed, Jojo jumped out of Simon's car. She turned around and looked at him. "Thanks. Sorry I have to go. Glad we could do this."

"Yeah, sure."

"But you'll get those tickets for me that we talked about."

Simon nodded and drummed his fingers on his steering wheel. "Hey, a deal's a deal. If I said I would get them for you, I'll get them for you."

"Great!" Jojo started to leave.

"But wait . . ." Simon called out.

Jojo turned around. She was impatient, but Simon was pointing a finger at her. "You just remember your part of the deal," he told her.

"You mean the hundred bucks?"

Simon winked, then he gunned his engine. "See ya," he called.

A moment later, Jojo was sitting beside her mother, who gazed at Jojo with her usual indulgent, loving smile.

"Hi, honey. I thought we'd stop downtown and get something new to wear," Mrs. Hernandez said. She frowned at Jojo's thrift-store skirt. "Jo, I have no idea why you bought that awful thing."

"I know you don't, Mom," Jojo answered.

"You don't understand what I'm going through. But you will."

"Oh, Jojo," her mother sighed. She started the Cadillac and checked the rearview mirror. "It'll be all right. You're not that hard to understand."

Jojo looked out the window. All the proud feeling had just leaked out of her. Sure, she'd stood up to Brandy. Yes, she was going to help Chip and Leanne. But if she didn't do something even more meaningful soon — something that her mother didn't understand — her life was still going to be a useless waste.

EIGHT

Leanne was an honorable person.

She'd been let down so many times that she'd vowed never to break a promise herself. But when she stared down at the pair of concert tickets in Chip's hands, she had to wonder if it wasn't time to change her code. Talk about impossible. She didn't want her honor to lead her into a horrendous trap.

"How did you get the tickets?" she gasped.

The two of them were standing outside the art room, next to a rack of clay sculptures drying in the sun. It was the break between sixth and seventh periods. People were whizzing by, and there wasn't much time.

Chip wore an exhilarated smile, as if the tickets had been handed to him by his fairy godmother. "They're for the late show. Saturday night at ten, the same night as the spirit dance. I know it's kind of short notice, but I still hope you can go. Oh. I got the tickets through my friends."

Friends. That figured. A trick like that could only be accomplished through friends. One was still the only number that Leanne trusted.

Chip just kept staring at her with his clear, hopeful eyes. She still couldn't believe that he even wanted to talk to her again after the way she'd been treating him. His expression was so sweet that Leanne had to look away.

When she didn't say anything Chip jumped in. "I don't mean to be so mysterious. Actually, Jojo got the tickets for me, from this other guy in our class. Amazing, huh?" He shrugged. "So do we have a date? You said we would. You don't have to go, but now that I have the tickets, I guess we should use them. It's up to you."

"A date?" Dates were for girls like Miranda Jamison, or Brandy Kurtz. The idea of "a date" was almost as impossible for Leanne as the other part of her bargain — showing up at those stupid talent show auditions after school that day. How had this happened to her?

"It doesn't have to be, like, a *date*, date," Chip clarified. "We could just go to the show together because we both want to go. We could even pretend we don't know each other and just sit at the same table." He smiled. "Well?"

Leanne still didn't answer him. Should she accept his end of the bargain — and *everything* that went with it — or tell him, "Get lost. Go jump. Whatever made you think I took you seriously?"

"What do you say?"

"I . . ." Leanne had to admit to herself that she'd taken Chip seriously — ever since the moment he'd invited her to Jojo's party. He'd always been there as the one person who might provide some light, some hope in her dingy life. He was the one guy who would never treat her the way Brent Tucker had. Thinking about Brent made her reconsider. Why had she been willing to listen to a snake like Brent, when she wouldn't even give Chip a chance?

Leanne was about to walk away, when someone rammed into her. An elbow stuck her in the back, and she let out an involuntary yelp. Then one of her high heels buckled, and she lunged forward, right at Chip who was carrying an armload of books.

Chip immediately reached out to steady her. One of his hands grabbed her shoulder, his other arm wove around her waist with gentleness and care. "Are you okay?" he cried as his books scattered across the walk. People stepped over the books and walked on his stuff, but Chip didn't seem to notice. His eyes were fixed on her.

For a moment Leanne was stuck on him, too. Rarely had she seen that kind of concern. Something inside her felt like it was being stripped away. She gazed back at Chip, for what seemed like a terrifyingly long time. When she felt something inside give way so that her knees almost buckled, she glanced down at a senior letterman who was stomping right on Chip's notebook.

"Hey! Watch what you're doing, you jerk!" she yelled at the senior jock.

Stunned, the jock looked at Leanne, then scrambled away.

Chip gathered his books and stood up.

She handed him his notebook. "Are you all right?"

"I'm okay. Whoa! That was great the way you yelled at that guy." Chip squinted to look after the jock, who had since disappeared. "I never do stuff like that."

"I never *don't* do stuff like that," Leanne admitted. "He'll probably tell the principal and have me sent to detention. I've heard that VP Hud is on a real tear. I'm sure I'll be the scapegoat. That's how things usually work out for me."

"But that guy *was* being a jerk."

"There are lots of jerks in this world."

The connection between them hooked up again. Leanne still didn't trust it. She tapped Chip's sleeve, then backed away. "So I guess I'll see you . . . sometime."

"Those auditions are today," Chip reminded.

"I know!" she snapped, stopping any further discussion of the talent show.

He took one step toward her, then a few steps back. He seemed to want to follow her but he also seemed to have a class in the opposite direction. "What about the concert? Should I call — ?"

"I'll call you," Leanne blurted out, cutting him off. " 'Bye." Then she left quickly because she didn't want to open up anymore. One thing led to another. Chip knew that she lived on her own, but he didn't know much more than that. Innocent questions about the concert would lead to the subject of getting off early from her job and why she had to have a job in the first place. That would lead to lots more why's and what happened's, and a lot of confessions that might make Chip think that everyone else was right — Leanne Heard deserved everything that had happened to her.

Maybe it wasn't her fault, Leanne considered, as she made her way to the gym. She couldn't help it if her mother didn't care enough to side with her and kick her boyfriend out. But then again, maybe her mother didn't care because Leanne wasn't worth caring about. And yet . . . Chip knew a few things about her, and he didn't look at her any differently.

"Nobody can be that nice," Leanne said to herself, as she hurried past the guidance office and the activity bulletin board. "If he was really that nice, why would he be interested in me?"

As Leanne approached the gym, that question kept bouncing back and forth in her head. Sometimes she felt like she was better than everyone else at school — wiser and more experienced, more independent and truly free. After all, what would Jojo or Lisa Avery do if they were suddenly on their own, without a penny from Mom and Dad? Would they have been able to survive like she had?

But as often as not, Leanne's feelings swung the other way. She could feel worthless and without hope, as if all she should ever expect was a crummy job washing dishes, and guys like Brent Tucker treating her any way they pleased.

Leanne pushed her way into the locker room.

As soon as she heard the echoey female voices and the slapping of tennis shoes along the cement floor, she went back into "school mode." She went throught the motions, watched and listened, but never really took part. Staring straight in front of her, she stepped over the center bench and opened her locker. She turned her back to the others, so that no one could see her worn underwear or know that even her gym suit had been bought secondhand.

After that, gym class was a stomach-churning blur. Leanne barely knew what team she was on, or the names of the other girls. They played soccer, and Leanne tried to get by with as little running and kicking as she could. But for once, her mind was focused on something besides what the other girls were saying and how to keep her distance from it all. During the game, the tune and lyrics to "Saturday's Girl" played over and over in her mind.

By the time Leanne left the shower, she was mouthing the lyrics nonstop and moving to the beat. She left the gym with the flow of the other girls, but didn't head off campus. Instead, she crossed the quad, walking twice around a trash can for luck, up two steps and quickly down again. She knocked on each of the library windows, then went back to tap the last one three more times until she reached the auditorium.

There was a crowd at the door and a bunch of kids lingering outside. Leanne stopped. She put on another layer of lipstick and the rice powder she used on her face. She went over her song again. It was all there. Every word. Every note.

She slunk into the auditorium. Auditions were already going on, and everyone was watching two guys doing a comedy routine. Leanne signed up, then skirted past Kat and Gabe, who were laughing too hard to notice her. She didn't see Chip, but couldn't miss Miranda. She was sitting in front with the judging committee, including Jackson Magruder, who had once given Leanne advice on getting her part-time job.

Like a ghost, Leanne floated up the aisle, taking in the rest of the crowd. She passed two of her least favorite Crescent Bay High social stars — Lisa Avery and cheerleader Brandy Kurtz, dressed in identical tights, crop tops, and leg warmers. Even though the comedy audition was still going on, their mouths were flapping.

"Did you love that public spat between Miranda and Jackson at the meeting?" Lisa was saying. "Was that outrageous or what? If everyone still thinks that Miranda is so perfect they'd better have their heads examined."

"Well, we don't have to worry about how she judges," Brandy assured Lisa. "Our dance number is only the best thing anyone will see all day."

"Tell me about it."

Tuning their mindless chatter out again, Leanne trudged all the way to the last row, where she sat hidden by the shadow of the balcony. From there, she waited nervously while people sang, emoted, told jokes, and played flutes and guitars. Brandy and Lisa did their dance routine. Their performance was impressive, mostly for sheer glitz and confidence.

"LEANNE HEARD," Miranda called out after Lisa and Brandy took their bow.

Heads turned. Lisa whispered something to Brandy as they trotted off the stage, and Brandy whispered something back.

Leanne slowly began to walk, feeling as if she were marching to the guillotine. She heard the echo of her own footsteps as she climbed onto the stage and approached Andrea Schumacher, the junior who was playing the piano. Leanne remembered Andrea from the only other time she'd ever tried out for anything else at school. She'd tried out for chamber singers early that

fall, been accepted, then backed out when she'd
decided to leave home.

"I didn't bring any music," Leanne confessed.

Suddenly Lisa giggled loudly, then was
shushed by Brandy, who giggled, too. Andrea
came to Leanne's defense. "I can play a lot of
things by ear. What do you want to sing?" Shy
and overweight, Andrea was also a very good
musician.

"Do you know 'Saturday's Girl'?"

"The Lara O'Toole song? I love her." Andrea
started playing the introduction, fairly close to
the way it sounded on the record.

Leanne found her way to the center of the
stage. Suddenly her hands felt like lead weights,
and her legs were wobbly. She wanted to run,
to scream, to do anything but sing her favorite
song for her stupid school.

Andrea had to play the intro twice before
Leanne figured out where to start. Amazingly,
when she opened her mouth, sound came out
and the very act of singing made her feel
more relaxed. By accident, she glanced briefly
at Jojo, who was in the third row, gazing up
with something that looked like admiration.
That was when she spotted him. Chip was
sitting next to Jojo, his chin resting in his hands,

his glasses on, his full attention on Leanne.

Leanne continued the song with her eyes closed. She pretended that she was home alone, sitting on her single bed in her rented room. She snapped her fingers. She swayed. She didn't worry about how she looked or what people thought. She felt her voice fill her, reflecting her anger and her strength.

At the end of the first verse, there was a break in the music. When Leanne came to that part, she stopped, just like Lara did on the record. She counted three beats in her head. One . . . two . . . But as she was taking her breath to resume the song, she heard a squeal of laughter explode in the auditorium.

"Maybe Leanne should put out a rock video," one girl giggled sarcastically.

"Only if she shaved her head," said the other.

"Who would notice? She already looks so spooky."

Leanne knew those voices as well as if she'd been blind. Lisa Avery and Brandy Kurtz.

They kept laughing. Sputter, sputter. Tee, hee, hee.

Leanne froze.

Miranda suddenly stood up and pointed a finger at the girls until they shut up.

"Go on, Leanne," Miranda said.

Leanne closed her hands into fists. Andrea was waiting for a cue to resume playing. Chip was jogging down the aisle now, as if he would leap onto the stage, scoop Leanne up in his slender arms, and carry her away.

Leanne took it all in. Lisa and Brandy. Miranda and the bizarre collection of judges marking little notes in little pads. Chip and Jojo and the old auditorium walls covered with murals of ships and waves. Then she said in a low voice, "This is a joke. Forget it. FORGET YOU ALL!"

Chip was a joke, too, she decided as she rushed off the stage, pushed open the side door, and ran out. And the way he'd talked her into trying out for their stupid talent show was the biggest, nastiest and most dangerous joke of all.

"Leanne's audition was . . . interesting," Miranda commented later when they were going over the list of talent show hopefuls in the auditorium foyer.

"Interesting can mean a lot of things," Jackson shot back. "It can mean provocative and different, or it can mean I don't have the guts to say how I really feel, so I'll call it *interesting*."

"Fine, Jackson," Miranda argued. "You watched Leanne's audition, too. I mean, she has a good voice, but her attitude is . . . well . . . What did you think?"

"No, Miranda," Jackson said. "Not just me. Not just you. What did we all think?"

"Okay," Miranda repeated, taking up his dare again and including the entire judging committee. "What did we all think?"

Three drama kids shook their heads. Two preppie types shrugged. But the rest of the committee, the loners and the misfits that Jackson had scrounged together, nodded and smiled.

In Miranda's opinion, the group of judges wasn't just diverse, it was intentionally weird. On the fringe, as her father would say. It reminded her of the collection of kids who were part of Friends in Need, the school's peer counseling program. Miranda understood the need to make the Friends in Need counselors diverse — after all, the kids who needed counseling were likely to be outside the mainstream. But this talent show was for the spirit drive. School spirit wasn't about pierced noses and pink hair. And Jackson's objections weren't about the spirit drive, either. This was all about Jackson proving that she was afraid to let fringe people participate. But that was okay. However far he dared her, she could take an even bigger risk.

Jackson took the floor again. "Especially since we decided to include Lisa and Brandy, I think we should give Leanne a real chance. Not that Lisa and Brandy's dance number wasn't good, but I want to balance things out."

"Jackson," Miranda stated, "this is a talent show, not a math problem."

"Miranda, you're the one who wants to treat everything like a math problem," he bantered. "X equals Y. Spirited attitude equals talent. I think Leanne showed a lot of talent, and a lot of guts to stand up to those girls today."

As opposed to me, who has no guts, Miranda thought. Every thing Jackson said, every look he cast her way, was a challenge. Are you brave enough, Miranda? Are you open-minded? Or are you just rigid Miranda who wimps out whenever things get tough? Just like you wimped out on me. On us.

"Fine," Miranda said. "Let's vote."

Hands went up. A few abstained. Miranda cast the deciding vote.

Leanne was in the show.

NINE

Chip tapped Jojo on the arm. "Thanks again for those concert tickets," he said. "If you hadn't gotten those, Leanne would never had tried out, and then she could never have gotten picked. Man, I wish I could have seen her face when that talent show list went up. As soon as I'm sure she's off work tonight, I'm going to go and see her. I'll bet she feels great!"

Jojo actually smiled. "So maybe my afternoon with Simon Wheeldon wasn't such a waste. At least I only have to see him one more time."

"It was all for a good cause, Jo," said Gabe. "Chip and Leanne Heard. What a pair. If this works out, it'll be amazing."

The three of them were at the Wave Cafe — their usual hangout, located down on the Crescent Bay pier. On one side of the restaurant there was an aquarium with a tiny mermaid sur-

rounded by a school of fish. On the other side
of the aquarium, Brent Tucker sat, eavesdrop-
ping. Brent was in a booth, where he could see
the trio through the aquarium's bubbly green
water.

"Where's Kat?" Jojo asked.

Brent perked up. *He* knew where Kat was.
She'd taken one look at him waiting by his BMW
and had raced back onto campus, probably to
pound nails for that dumb talent show. She'd
suddenly acted like a school talent show was
more important than Brent Tucker! He'd bared
his soul to her, and she was avoiding him. Since
he'd found her in the costume storage room, she
always seemed to be with Gabe or Miranda. He
really *was* going to have to wait for that dorky
spirit dance, where there'd be a ton of people
around showing off new dance steps and voting
on the battle of the bands.

Brent tuned into Chip, Gabe, and Jojo again.

"At least you're here," Chip said to Jojo. He
nudged her. "I thought maybe you'd given up
Wave Burgers."

"It was either come here or go shopping with
my mom," Jojo said.

Gabe pretended to faint. "Jojo, we're hon-
ored."

Jojo threw a french fry at him. "I don't know what to do about her. I wish she took me seriously."

"We take you seriously," Gabe assured her, "even though you're kind of acting like Dr. Jekyll or Mr. Hyde — I can't remember which. Hey, Jo, since you're the expert in personality changes, will you tell me something?"

Jojo looked up.

"Do you think Kat's acting different lately?" Gabe asked. "Especially since the day we cleaned the auditorium."

Brent perched forward.

"I mean, she started acting differently toward me after I had to pick her up the night of your party," Gabe went on. "But she's been even stranger since we cleaned the aud. Has she said anything about feeling different, or wanting to hang around me more?"

"Watch it," Chip teased. "And you make fun of me and Leanne."

"Jojo knows Kat and I are just friends," Gabe assured him. Then he stared down at his soda. "At least I think we are. Maybe I'm not sure anymore."

"And maybe that's part of the problem," said Chip.

You bet it's a problem, Brent wanted to scream as he stared around the fish and the tiny swaying plants. He was beginning to wonder if Kat's stupid friends weren't his problem, too. Especially now that he knew that Gabe was part of the picture, and that sleazy, sexy Leanne had joined their clan. *Leanne!* Until Kat had shut him down, Leanne had been the one girl he'd run into since moving to Crescent Bay that really bugged him. He'd gone out of his way to be nice to her when she was just a lowlife. And now she was trying to make something of herself . . . trying to be a school star.

Brent sat back in the booth and shook his head. No way was he going to let himself fall while Leanne and Gabe rose. If he couldn't get Kat, he certainly wasn't going to sit around and watch Leanne — or any of Kat's friends — swim to the top of the Crescent Bay waters.

"Come on, come on. Be home, Leanne. Be home."

After leaving Gabe and Jojo at the Wave, Chip listened to the radio, while tapping the steering wheel of his van. He drummed off the seconds until he was sure that Leanne could be home from work. He'd been aching to share her moment of triumph with her.

Chip thought back to Leanne's audition that afternoon. Boy, he'd admired the way Leanne had told Lisa and Brandy off. He wished that every once in a while he could tell bullies and brats to SHUT UP. But as his van chugged through downtown, he had to admit that his way would have been to ignore the insults, to smile and promote peaceful good cheer.

"Four thirteen Norton Street," he recited, checking Leanne's address of the scrap of paper Jojo had given him.

He turned off Ocean Avenue. Tourist boutiques and motels turned to a boat repair shop, a supermarket, and some warehouses. Jojo had said that Leanne's room was in a creepy part of Crescent Bay, but Chip never saw one part of town as being better than any other. He lived in a new housing tract near the golf club, where every house looked so much alike that he sometimes went to the wrong door.

He appreciated the old buildings that had been turned into rooming houses, with their carved window frames and front stoops. Chip parked right in front. The street was deserted, and Leanne's building was made of gray brick. He pushed in the street door, entering a stuffy foyer lined with doorbells and mailboxes. Quickly he found Leanne's buzzer, but before he pressed it, an old man shuffled out, so Chip slipped in unannounced. He bolted up two flights of stairs, taking three steps with each stride, until he found Leanne's floor. He found six doors, looking all the same. It took him a moment to find Leanne's, and then he pounded and sang out with excitement.

"Leanne! It's me, Chip. Chip Kohler. You know. Is it too late?"

He held his smile and waited for her door to fly open. His excitement built as he waited to see her lush, pale face.

No answer.

Chip checked the number on the door, then knocked again. "Leanne! I'm sorry I didn't call first, but Jojo told me you just have a phone down the hall so I figured I wouldn't be able to reach you anyway. Are you home?"

Still nothing.

"LEANNE! IT'S ME! CHIP!"

Chip felt a nasty twinge. He wondered if Leanne was out with someone else and remembered gossip about how she threw herself at the guys she worked with. He knew that none of that could possibly be true, and yet a part of him was already preparing for the inevitable — that Leanne would keep playing him for a fool.

Still, Chip didn't want to lump Leanne in the category with all his other hopeless crushes. Of course, he also knew that he might be setting himself up for his biggest fall yet.

Chip needed to think things over, so he flopped down on the hall floor, which was made of cold black-and-white tiles. He'd been there a few minutes, his head in his hands, when he heard two locks clunk. There was a squeak, and then Leanne's door slowly opened.

Chip was telling himself to be cool, but he'd already jumped up to meet her. He caught a glimpse of her room. A thin bed, a rickety dresser, a lamp, and pictures from magazines taped to the wall.

"I thought you'd left," Leanne grumbled. She didn't sound excited or triumphant. If anything, she was even more sullen than usual. She closed the door a little to block any further view of her room. "Did you come to see where I live, so you can make fun of me, too? Or did you want to dare me to come to some other stupid thing at school so that everyone could laugh at me?"

Everything about her stunned him. Her hair

was tied back in a sloppy ponytail, and she wore a big white T-shirt over torn sweats. Her eyes were puffy, and her mouth was pale. It was the first time Chip had seen her without her dark red lipstick, and he was amazed to see how young and frail she looked.

"Leanne . . ."

"I don't want to see you," she told him, biting her lip and fighting tears. "Go away!"

"Me?"

"GO AWAY!" she screamed. Then she turned and started to close the door in his face.

Chip felt as if the wind had been knocked out of him. He and Leanne hadn't been doing too well before this, but now it was out-and-out war. He stood there, speechless, barely breathing, as an old woman from across the hall unlocked her door and glared at them.

"Mrs. Mullen," Leanne gasped.

"I'm trying to sleep!" Mrs. Mullen barked. "Be quiet."

Leanne quickly stepped into the hall. Her room door closed behind her. "I'm sorry."

"Don't let it happen again." Mrs. Mullen slipped back into her room again.

Leanne collapsed back against her room door and pointed at Chip. "I'm already behind in my rent, Chip. All I need is for Mrs. Mullen to complain. All I need is for you to get me kicked out of my room!"

"But you're the one who yelled," Chip said.

"Well, you're the one who made me stand in front of everyone at school so they could all laugh at me."

"What?"

She began crying, and Chip instantly felt like crying, too. She turned her back on him, but he couldn't stand seeing her shudder and gasp, so he stepped forward and tapped her shoulder. When she didn't respond, he took a deep breath. He wasn't sure whether to shake her or walk away. So he tentatively wrapped his arms around her, feeling her soft arms push against him.

"I hate you," she said, shoving him with her elbow. "I hate all of you."

For some reason, he just held her more tightly. He didn't apologize or ask permission. He just clutched her, almost pinning her arms until he felt her body relax. She stood quietly against him. He felt a few tears soak his T-shirt.

"I don't hate *you*," he said. "I . . ." He ran out of nerve and didn't say anything else.

"What a joke," she scoffed. "What a stupid

joke." Then her knees buckled, and she folded onto the hard tile. He crumpled down next to her. They sat there like that, just listening to one another breathe while the overhead lights buzzed and someone clomped around on the floor below.

"Why are you here?" she finally asked in a belligerent voice. "Why do you keep bothering with me?"

"Just patient, I guess," he said. "Or maybe dense. Dumb. It's a family trait."

"Family," Leanne grumbled. "I have this vision of your family as these super-nice people who smile all the time, and have talks around the kitchen table . . . like on TV."

"Right," he scoffed. "The Kohler Bunch."

She wiped her face with the heel of her palm.

"Actually, I sometimes think there's too much niceness at my house," Chip considered. "Nobody ever yells. If you get mad in my family, you have to, like, count to ten, take deep breaths, and then have a reasonable discussion. That's probably why I'm so thoughtful and decent. Of course, the flip side is that girls think nothing of telling me off and slamming doors in my face."

She glanced up at him. "I wouldn't mind living someplace where no one ever yells. Every time my mom's boyfriend said something to me, he yelled. And I yelled back."

"That's why you moved away?" Chip asked.

"He hit me, too."

Chip didn't know how to react. The idea of hitting anyone made him sick to his stomach.

Leanne stared at the floor. "He gave me a black eye, and I didn't go to school for six days. Then I told my mother I wanted to move out."

"Did your mom freak?"

"I think she was relieved."

They sat a while in silence again. For a long time neither of them moved until Chip slowly let his head fall onto her shoulder. Even though he wanted to comfort her, to be the strong one who would make it all better, he was stunned to hear what she'd been through. He felt her hand slip into his, and his heart seemed to stop as she turned her face toward him.

For a moment she pressed her cheek to his — Chip felt as if he were suspended in midair. Then she kissed his cheek. Nothing more. It was a short, light kiss, barely a flutter of her lips against his skin, but it made Chip woozier than if he'd leaned over the balcony of an eighty-story building. He clutched her hand, then kissed her shoulder through her T-shirt and almost started crying himself.

"You'd better go," she said, glancing at Mrs. Muller's door again. She pulled her hand out of his and stood up.

Still in a warm, blurry haze, Chip stumbled to his feet, too. He took a step toward the stairs, then turned back. "What about the concert?" he had to ask. "Will you still go?"

"I don't owe you anything anymore." She put her hands on her hips, falling back into her old defensiveness. "Not after the way that audition turned out."

Finally it dawned on him. She didn't know that she'd made it into the show after all! "You don't know, do you?"

"Know what?"

"Didn't you check the talent show list after school today?"

"I had to go right to work at the resort."

"But you made it," he blurted out. "They picked you. You're in. You have one rehearsal for everybody next week, and then you're on."

"What?"

Something amazing had suddenly happened to Leanne's face. For a split second, all the sul-

lenness and pain disappeared. Her eyes bright-
ened. Her cheeks flushed. "Are you serious?"
she asked in an almost innocent voice. "You're
not being warped or handing me some kind of
line?"

"Not me." He grinned.

"But why? Why would they have picked me?"

"I guess you were good."

She put her hands together and leaned her head
back, as if something beautiful were painted on
the grimy ceiling. Soon Chip began to laugh,
laugh so loudly that Mrs. Mullen would probably complain again. Leanne actually laughed,
too. So they both tried to laugh quietly, which
made their laughter turn to silly gasps and sput-
ters and tiny squeaky sounds that sent happy
tears down their cheeks.

Finally Mrs. Mullen thumped on the inside of
her door and Leanne held a finger to her lips.

Chip nodded and whispered. "What about
Saturday night? If you don't want to go, I guess
I could go to the spirit dance instead. But I'd
hate to waste those tickets."

She shrugged. "I'll have to get off work
early."

"You could work until nine or so, and then
just meet me in front of the club. The show

doesn't start until ten. Just meet me in front of the club before ten. I'll be waiting for you."

"You are weird, too, you know."

"I know."

"Finally, you have the nerve to admit it." She bobbed forward and kissed his cheek. He kissed her forehead. She kissed his hand. He kissed her hair. Then they embraced one another, quickly, almost frantically, until she let him go, and he leaped back down the stairs.

Chip wasn't sure how he made it down the steps and back to his van. He didn't know how he made it home. All he knew was that somehow he got back to his house without thinking about anything other than Leanne.

TEN

"Let's hear it for all the bands that played for our spirit dance tonight!"

"YAAAAAYYYYYYYYY!"

"Now we'll vote on a winner so we can all get back on the dance floor."

"That's right, Kat. Rock 'til you roll."

"Shuffle and bustle."

"Shake and bake."

"Hip hop 'til you drop."

"Boogie 'til you barf."

"*Boogie 'til you barf?* Oh, Gabe. Yuuuuk."

Kat and Gabe were poised on either side of the platform that had been set up on the gym floor. They were finishing their routine after the battle of the bands for the spirit dance. It was one of those times when they were really clicking together. No glitches. No dead air. No worries about jokes falling flat or missing one another's cues.

"Now that the bands have battled . . ." Gabe pointed out.

Kat cut in. ". . . and we have it down to two final finalists."

Gabe smiled. "It's time for you, the audience . . ."

Kat smiled back. "To vote . . ."

". . . with your applause."

Kat held up her hands. "To judge your response, we are going to use the KHOT human applause meter!"

She and Gabe raced toward the middle of the stage, pretended to knock heads, then wound their arms like pitching machines. Finally they both fell onto their backs and stuck their feet in the air like bugs.

Everyone laughed.

Kat jumped up again. "Who votes for Crescent Bay High's favorite all-girl group, Jane Flash!"

Gabe swung his arms. "It's almost off the meter!" he yelled.

Then he sprung up and Kat flopped down, sitting on the edge of the stage, her arms posed to the meter this time.

"Let's hear it for Fire Fly, Crescent Bay High's only rap/salsa/singalong group," Gabe encouraged.

Kat trembled and strained as the crowd screamed louder and stomped their feet. Finally she fell off the edge of the platform.

"Fire Fly did it!" Gabe screamed, as he reached down to help Kat back up. "Come on up, guys, and take a bow. Play us one last rap singalong."

The four seniors who made up Fire Fly raced to the stage and grabbed their instruments, launching into a rap version of the school song. Kids stomped their feet and rapped along.

Kat grabbed Gabe's hand and pulled him away from the limelight. The two of them rested on the corner of the bleachers, sharing a watery Coke.

"Good gig," she said.

"Ditto, dudette." Gabe smiled.

Kat watched the crowd hopping around and having a great time. She was in the mood to cut loose and get silly, because she was starting to feel as if she were in a pressure cooker — one owned and operated by Brent Tucker. The whole time she'd been cutting up onstage with Gabe, Brent had been watching her. He was still there, leaning against the side wall, so still that he might have been painted on a billboard. His arms were folded in a sport coat and dark turtleneck, his legs were crossed in neat tan slacks. Kat watched as Brandy Kurtz strode up to Brent and seemed to be asking him to dance. But Brent just shook his head and kept his eyes on Kat.

Kat inched even closer to Gabe. "Is Chip here?" she asked. A tiny part of her was till flattered by Brent's crazy attentions, but a bigger part of her was getting the royal creeps.

Gabe shook his head. "Tonight's Chip's big date with Leanne."

"Oh, right."

"He's not meeting Leanne until late, but when I called him, he was already vacuuming out his van."

"I hope he doesn't change his clothes ten times," Kat joked.

"I don't think Chip owns ten changes of clothes."

Kat nodded. Brent was moving, slowly making his way through the crowd.

Just as Kat reached out to cling to Gabe, a pretty sophmore named Alexis White popped out of the crowd and threw herself into Gabe's lap.

"How come you're not dancing, Gabe?" Alexis flirted.

Instead of flirting back, Gabe hesitated. He gave Kat a "save me" look. But Alexis didn't notice.

"Come on," Alexis teased. She grabbed both of Gabe's hands and dragged him onto the floor. Gabe took one last look back at Kat, and then was swallowed up by the bouncing, gyrating crowd.

Even though the gym was jam-packed, Kat suddenly felt very alone. Miranda was manning the door, busily counting the money. Jojo had stayed home. By the time Kat realized that there was no one to cling to, nowhere to hide, Brent was standing right in front of her.

"Oh. Hi," Kat breathed. She stood up. His eyes were like two chips of blue ice.

Without taking his eyes off her, he reached down and placed his palm against hers, raising their hands and lacing fingers. "Let's dance," he ordered.

"I look kind of dorky," Kat said, hoping to make a joke. She was referring to her battle of the bands outfit, an old marching-band coat and Crescent Bay High baseball cap.

Brent reached forward and the scent of his after-shave made her dizzy. He took off her cap and placed it on the bleacher, then he peeled off her band coat, making her turn around as he let it fall from her shoulders. Facing him again, Kat felt almost naked in her walking shorts, vest, and T-shirt.

Brent led her to a dimly lit corner of the gym floor. Just then, Fire Fly launched into their one slow song, a blues number with lots of harmonica. Kat held her arms for a formal dance position, but right away he slid both hands around her waist and pulled her in close. She had no choice but to gingerly place her arms around his neck.

Brent barely moved. He held her as if all he could think about was the feel of her body next to him. Meanwhile, Kat shuffled her feet and looked around, hoping to break Brent's mood by chatting with another couple. But it was the first slow song of the evening and everybody seemed pretty focused on his or her partner.

"I love you, Kat," Brent whispered again.

The first time that Brent had said it, Kat had melted. No guy had ever said that to her before, and those were heavy, important words.

But this time, those three syllables sounded like a threat.

"Brent, why do you keep saying that? You don't even know me."

"I know everything about you."

"You do not."

His cheek was right next to hers. His arms were anchored around her back, and his mouth was against her ear. "Yes I do," he breathed. "Kathleen McDonough. Aged sixteen. You have one brother named Sam, aged twelve. Your parents have turned your house into a bed-and-breakfast, renting rooms to tourists."

"Those are just facts. Everyone knows that. None of that says anything about who I am."

"Okay." He pulled her even closer. "You keep your history book in Jojo's locker. Miranda tutors you in algebra. When you leave for school in the morning, you usually forget something and your mother has to run after you with it. You have study hall third period, but you sneak into the library and read plays."

Kat stopped moving, too.

He nuzzled the side of her neck and kept on talking in a low, mesmerizing voice. "Your bed at home is a mattress on the floor, covered with a patchwork quilt. You have a poster of Lily Tomlin on your bedroom wall and another one of that swimmer, Janet Evans."

Kat was starting to get chills.

"You have a rocking chair in your room with an embroidered pillow on it that says, 'Don't make me laugh.' "

What was Brent going to do next — tell her what was in her underwear drawer? Kat's bedroom was on the second floor, so he couldn't have even peeped in. "How do you know all this?" Kat said in a worried voice.

"I just know."

She wrenched away from him and looked into his face. Fear was starting to well up deep in her stomach. "Brent. How do you know?"

One side of his mouth lifted in a proud smile. "I pretended to be a tourist checking out the McDonough B-and-B for my family's next vacation. Your father didn't suspect a thing. And when he left me to answer the phone, I took a little detour upstairs. Don't underestimate me, Kat."

"I don't," she breathed. "Believe me."

"I found out other things, too," Brent went on.

"What? How?"

"I talked to people. Mostly girls. I skipped your very best friends — I'll deal with them later — but I quizzed girls who knew you from drama and swimming. It's amazing the number of girls who like to talk to me."

Kat's stomach clenched. No wonder she'd been feeling so creepy lately. Brent had been following her every move.

Brent pulled her in again and whispered. "I know there's no other guy. At least not now. One girl on the swim team thought there was some guy last summer, but it didn't work out and it's definitely over now. Everybody talks about how you hang out with Gabe all the time, and no one's quite sure what's really between you two. But I'm not worried."

"You're not?"

"I can tell that you and Gabe are just friends."

In a panic, Kat tried to struggle away again, but Brent wouldn't let her. She looked for Gabe and spotted him under the basketball hoop, sneaking away from Alexis.

"Brent, I don't want to dance anymore," Kat said. She put her hand flat on his chest and tried to push him away, but he held her even more tightly. He nuzzled the side of her neck, then lightly kissed her ear. Her knees buckled. His hand worked its way under the back of her sweater and started to climb her bare back.

Kat wasn't sure what to do. Her head was light, and her legs were wobbly. Part of her wanted to slap Brent, to kick him out of her life for good, but another part of her was afraid that she might give in again. Out of the corner of her eye she saw Gabe again, forcing his way through the crowd with a worried expression.

Just then, Brent's arms relaxed, but Kat realized that he was only letting her pull back so that he could kiss her. Brent's eyes were closed. His lips were parted. As Brent craned his neck to reach her mouth, she gave him a fierce shove. The force made Kat stumble backward and fall into Gabe's arms.

"What's going on?" Gabe asked suspiciously, looking back and forth between Kat and Brent. He held Kat even more fiercely than Brent had.

"Leave us alone," Brent threatened.

"Gabe!" Kat was so happy to see Gabe that for some reason, without thinking, her lips pressed his and all her confusion, her faintheadedness, went into that kiss instead of the one with Brent. Gabe's arms felt so safe and so right. She'd just meant it to be a quick thank-you-you-saved-me kiss, but as soon as her lips

touched his, something changed. She relaxed.
Gabe pulled her closer. They both seemed to lose
track of everything for a minute and glide on
some breathless cloud where there was no Brent,
no dance, no gym, nothing but lips and hands
and an incredibly warm, frothy feeling.

And then it was over. Kat let Gabe go. He
staggered back with a stunned expression, and
she moved away, too.

At the same time, she remembered Brent.

Brent's face was frozen as if he were trying to
cast a spell on her. He started to say something,
then backed away in anger. He rammed into a
freshman, sending the kid to his knees. And
then, as Kat and Gabe stood breathlessly staring,
Brent left the gym.

It was always lonely to be on campus at night.
Even though the gym was lit up and Fire Fly's
rap lyrics could probably be heard on the football
field, Crescent Bay High was empty. It seemed
like a different planet.

After locking up the journalism room, Jackson
Magruder pulled his skateboard out of his locker
and tucked it under his arm. He listened to the
dim beat of the music, and wondered if he should
go over to the dance now that his newspaper

work was done. He wished that for once in his life he could have a simple, straightforward evening. No skateboarding on the prom and looking at the moon. No working late and thinking of new ideas for Crescent Bay High's *Bay News*. No stewing over what happened with Miranda and why he'd been unable to give things a second chance.

It *was* over. Jackson couldn't hold back or stay with someone who didn't face things head-on. Something in him felt that everything in the world was potentially dangerous. There was no avoiding it. If you ran away, it would just find you and blow up in your face.

He put his skateboard down and rode across the quad. *Swish. Churn. Whoosh.* He closed his eyes as the sound and the motion traveled through him. He saw the ground with his feet, until he opened his eyes again. He saw Miranda strolling on the same concrete path, with a metal box hanging from her hand and a lonely expression on her beautiful face.

Jackson dragged his toe and stopped. Miranda's step faltered, but she passed him by, just like she did at school these days. Not even a Hello, how are you? much less an acknowledgment that only a short time before they had been the most important people in one another's lives. Jackson felt an ache in the back of his throat and a cold, empty feeling that might turn to tears when he was finally alone.

"Miranda."

"Yes."

"It's me."

"I know."

Jackson flipped the skateboard off the ground and into his hand. He glanced back over his shoulder and saw her take two steps in his direction. He had the eerie sense that for that moment, at least, they were back on track.

"I'm going to take the dance money to the office," she said, barely looking at him.

"I was working late on an article for the paper," he said.

She turned all the way around. "You were pretty hard on me at that talent show meeting."

"I didn't mean to be," Jackson answered.

He hadn't wanted to push and challenge her all the time. Maybe it was something in him that was threatened by her sureness and her strength. Maybe he just wanted to force her to feel as unsure about things as he'd felt so much of the time. "Life is hard. School is hard," Jackson admitted. "If you think everything should be easy,

then you never get anywhere — at least not anywhere worth going."

"It's okay. Did you think that running off with
you was just easier than making a clean break
with Eric?" Miranda asked with surprising di-
rectness. "That wasn't easy at all. None of this
is easy for me."

"Me neither. I just know we have to keep at
it." He wanted to take her in his arms so much
that he had to look away. "I miss you so much.
But I can't go back if we're going to hide and
always take the easy way."

"I'm a lot more daring than you think, Jackson," she said. "At least I'm trying to be. I may
just surprise you one of these days."

"Please do."

She headed for the office while he dropped his
skateboard and glided out of her life again.

ELEVEN

Kat had kissed Gabe . . .

Deliberately. Right in front of him. Her hands going out, then her arms around Gabe's shoulders, and finally the kiss. Gabe closing his eyes, too, pulling Kat in close and looking like he would never let go.

Brent wanted to kill.

He couldn't stop seeing that kiss, even after he'd run out of the gym. Past the crowd lined up around the band. Past the teachers posted at the door. Past the kids talking in the hall. None of them mattered. The only person who had mattered in the whole crummy school was Kat.

Brent had broken out of the school building in a fury. In the parking lot he'd seen stars that looked cold and icy blue — just the opposite of the way he had felt. He'd climbed into his new BMW, the most extravagant car in the whole parking lot. But at first, he'd just sat there, feeling so depressed that it might as well have been a jalopy.

He'd offered himself to Kat. He'd said things to her that he'd never said to any other girl. And what had Kat done in return? She had betrayed him.

Finally Brent had pushed down hard on the accelerator and peeled out. He'd just wanted to hear the ocean breaking against the beach, the waves pounding against the sand. He'd wanted to find some relief for his terrible burning desire and rage.

A few minutes later he was standing on the prom between the ocean and his family's resort. The waves crashed and pounded. The salty air stung Brent's cheeks and eyes, but no more than the tears that had already trickled down.

Kat, Kat, how could you choose Gabe over me? Don't you see how much I want you? Don't you know who I am?

No, she didn't know. She never would. He'd done everything he could to prove himself, and she'd just thrown him away.

Brent turned around, shutting his mind off from the beauty of the ocean. He walked briskly to the entrance of the resort, pushed his way through the door, and stood in the lush, carpeted lobby. All around him overnight guests wore relaxed smiles and made pleasant conversation. Potted palms fluttered, and a string quartet played. Employees offered polite greetings and overeager smiles. All of it made Brent want to jump on top of the counters, to throw luggage across the lobby and scream.

Don't you all know what's going on inside me! I don't know how to get this out or to make it feel any better. I only know that I want to hurt someone else as much as Kat just hurt me.

But Brent didn't jump or scream or grab a bellhop by the collar. Even in his overpowering rage, Brent knew that he couldn't afford to make a scene. Not in the lobby, anyway. So he headed back toward the dining room kitchen. It was the one place where he could make as much commotion as he wanted. Someone screaming their guts out wouldn't matter if there were pots and pans banging around.

As soon as Brent got there, he smelled warm bread and the steamy combination of seafood and soup. The chefs were working at top speed, so he went further back to the room where they washed dishes and stored pots. As Brent stomped by, the hard tiles of the kitchen floor sent the same message to his brain. Don't take it. She's just a small-town girl with all her small-town friends. She has a lot of nerve turning you down after all the time and effort you put in.

The dishwashing room was empty. As soon as Brent was inside, he grabbed two pots from the overhead rack and threw them to the ground. No one reacted to the clangs and crashes, and he enjoyed the racket as he backed up against the door and kicked one of the pots against the wall. That's when one of the swinging doors flew open. It bumped against Brent's shoulder, making him give out a little yelp. "Hey!"

"Sorry."

"Well, what do you know. Look who's here."

"Get out of my way."

Leanne Heard was on the other side of the doorway wearing her weird kitchen suit and holding a big stainless-steel pot filled with soapy water. It was obviously heavy, and she was eager to get past him and set it down. Still she didn't move, but stood in the doorway daring him to move first.

"What do you think you're doing?" Brent asked her, feeling satisfaction for the first time that evening. Leanne was just the person he wanted to see. He suddenly realized that he'd probably come to the kitchen in search of her again.

"I'm working. What does it look like I'm doing?" She blew a damp string of hair off her face. "Do you mind? I said I'm sorry."

"You'd better be." They glared at each other. Brent had been on such good behavior when he'd seen her in the dressing room. But that was a lifetime ago, when he still thought there might be a reward for being trustworthy and nice.

Brent finally stepped aside and let Leanne stagger to put down the heavy pot. Some of the soapy water splashed in her face. Immediately, he followed her, coming up close and pinning her against the counter.

"What are you doing when you finish work?" he asked.

She tried to stab him with her elbow, but he caught her arm and held it tight. "I'm leaving early tonight," she said. "I get off in a few minutes, and I'd like to finish this."

"Why are you leaving early? Got a hot date?"

"Maybe I do. It's no business of yours."

"You *do* have a date, don't you? Well, what do you know."

She tried to squeeze away from him, and Brent remembered Chip. The thought of that long-haired wimp together with Leanne made Brent want to smash that whole crowd against a concrete wall. He wished he could go through that crowd one by one and make each of them squirm and pay.

Brent was just about to press Leanne again, when Stacy Woolf, the dining room manager, stuck her head in. Stacy was in her twenties and eager to get ahead. She was one of the many employees that treated Brent like some kind of demigod just because he was the bosses' son.

"Hi, Brent," Stacy said brightly.

Brent turned on his friendly voice. "Stace, how are you?"

Leanne turned away, as if she wanted to hide in the dishwashing machine.

"Just fine, and you?" Stacy answered in her A-in-Hotel-Management style. She wore a salmon-colored Tucker Resort blazer with a name tag and little scarf.

"I'm great," Brent lied. "Just great."

Stacy's smile lingered on him. Then she leaned in and pointed to Leanne. "Leanne, you can go. I know you need to get somewhere. It's almost nine, and John MacDiarmid is here to cover for you."

Leanne gave a sullen nod.

Stacy smiled at Brent one more time before moving on to look in on the chefs.

As soon as Stacy was gone, Leanne spun back to face Brent. "Just let me get out of here in peace," Leanne threatened before he could say anything. "I don't want to hassle with you tonight. I have to meet someone important, and I don't want to be late."

If she didn't want to be late, then late was exactly what Brent wanted her to be. He backed into the doorway, blocking the exit and daring her with his eyes. She hesitated, then tried to storm past him. He laughed. It was like a game of keepaway. Every time she moved, he blocked her. He stuck out his hands, landing light slaps on her arms. When he saw her face begin to redden and her eyes fill with rage, he leaned in and landed a slap right on her left cheek.

She let out a little cry and put her hand to her face. He watched her eyes glaze over with hate and humiliation, and he knew he had her exactly where he wanted her.

"I hate you," she seethed, turning back toward the kitchen and picking up something out of a nearby tray.

Brent almost laughed, but before it could

come out of his mouth, a dish came flying at him, smashing into his chest, dripping some kind of red, smelly sauce down the front of his shirt.

Brent's first reaction was to grab Leanne, to rub the sauce all over her, to send her on her big date with dried tomato matted on her hair. But he reminded himself of his best interests, his real chance for revenge.

"You asked for it, Leanne," he whispered. Then he leaned into the hall and raised his voice. "STACY, COULD YOU COME BACK HERE?"

Leanne looked at him, her gray eyes wide as two stones. A moment later, Stacy was at the door again with her name tag and professional smile. As soon as she saw the mess on Brent's shirt, she gasped as if it were a gunshot wound.

"Brent, what happened?"

"Your employee just had a little temper tantrum," Brent explained in his coolest voice.

Leanne refused to look at either of them.

"Apparently Leanne doesn't like this job," Brent explained. "She just told me she lied about having a reason to get off early, Stace. The real truth is that Leanne just doesn't want to work.

And when I told her I didn't think that was a great attitude, she decided to take her frustration out on me."

"Leanne!" Stacy snapped. She handed Brent a clean dish towel.

Brent dabbed at his shirt. "Leanne's trouble, Stace. My dad's been complaining about her. He's wanted to fire her a few times. I just came in to try and clear things up."

"Leanne, what do you have to say for yourself?" Stacy demanded.

Leanne glared at Stacy, just the way Brent hoped she would.

Stacy seemed to have a moment of doubt or indecision. She looked back and forth from Brent to Leanne. Then Brent gave her his best Boy Scout expression while Leanne continued to glare.

"Leanne," Stacy finally said with a resigned sigh. "You're fired. I'm sorry, but I don't have any choice. You can pick up your final paycheck anytime next week." Stacy shook her head and then walked away.

Brent waited until Stacy was long gone, then offered a smug smile.

"Why did you do that?" Leanne managed. "I can't survive without this job."

"I just did it for fun," Brent gloated.

Tears began to run down her cheeks. "I should have known something like this would happen," she cried. She shoved Brent with her shoulder before she hurried past him. "I should have known my luck would never change."

Brent stayed in the dishwashing pit for a long time. Leanne had hit him hard, but that was all right. He would have another chance. He wasn't through. Brent wasn't through with any of them.

I know. This is really corny. But I can't help it, Chip thought, as he stood in front of the Blue Cove Music Club. Maybe I'm just a corny guy.

Waiting for Leanne, he clutched a single red rose, bought from the street vendor near the freeway offramp. Chip knew he should probably break the stem and pin the rose to his vest, or just stick it into an empty pop bottle and leave it somewhere. But he didn't want to. Okay, it *was* corny. But he wanted to present it to Leanne. He wanted to hold it out to her as soon as she arrived and see the delighted look on her face.

Chip pulled out his pocket watch, then dropped it back into his jeans. "Ten minutes 'til," he reminded himself.

While he waited, people rushed past him, scurrying into the club. Happy, eager fans bursting at the seams to see Lara O'Toole in the flesh. Chip was eager, too, but not about seeing Lara O'Toole. He just wanted to see Leanne again, to get to know her better and find out where they were headed next.

As the minutes ticked off, Chip sniffed the rose and moved out of the flow of traffic. Most of the people had already gone inside, and it seemed like the show was about to start. The taped music had been turned off, and musicians were warming up. There was the twang of an electric guitar. A few flicks on a drum. The hum of a microphone and a smattering of applause.

Chip shifted. He smoothed his hair. He checked his pocket watch again. He wasn't worried. After all, Leanne had to get off work, then probably change her clothes. He realized that he should have arranged to pick her up and wondered if he should call the Tucker Resort to make sure she'd got out of there on time.

Instead, he kept waiting. A full half hour later, he could faintly hear Lara's opening set through the club's closed doors. The street was deserted. The fog was starting to roll in. Chip watched the occasional car cruise by with a sick feeling in his stomach, as if someone had sucker-punched him, then laughed and run away.

"How long are you going to wait?" he finally asked himself. "All night? All year? The rest of your life?"

"Some people are so slow," he muttered as he kicked the sidewalk and finally walked back to his van. His limbs were weary, as if the life had been drained out of them. After all he and Leanne had been through — all the hesitations and false starts and the doubts, she'd let him down, like every other girl. A tiny part of him still wasn't willing to give up, though. There could have been a reason, he told himself. If something had happened, Leanne couldn't have reached him. Maybe she had gotten sick or lost or mixed up about the time.

Chip drove to her rooming house, got out, and paced up and down her street. He saw a light on in her room; at least, he thought it was her room. He actually walked up and opened the door to the foyer, then backed out and closed it again.

Didn't he have any pride at all?

"Not much," he grumbled as he paced back

to the corner and stepped into a phone booth. He punched the number of the pay phone on Leanne's floor.

"Yeah," answered the woman Chip recognized as Mrs. Mullen, Leanne's neighbor who'd spied on them in the hall.

"Can I speak to Leanne? It's her friend, Chip."

"Yeah."

Chip heard flip-flops slap against tile. Mrs. Mullen yelled to Leanne. A door opened, then slammed shut again.

"Leanne's here," Mrs. Mullen said when she came back to the phone. "But she doesn't want to talk to you. Stop bothering us."

"Right." Chip hung up the receiver and felt as if he were putting his heart on hold. What had he done to deserve such treatment? Was this what he got for being so mellow and nice?

Chip became aware of a fiery feeling deep in his chest. He tried taking deep breaths. He told himself to ignore the feeling until it went away. But when none of the tricks would work, he threw Leanne's red rose into the gutter and angrily climbed into his van.

TWELVE

It rained all day Monday. It was one of those days where the ocean, the wet air, the sand, and mushy grass all seemed to goop together. Crescent Bay felt like one big marsh.

"Let's get this over with," Jojo said. She sat in Simon's car after school, staring at the soggy shops on Ocean Avenue. Awnings dripped. Windows were steamed over. Sidewalk displays had been covered with plastic or taken down.

"If you ask me, you got this over with before we even started," Simon complained. He blew a curl of red hair off his forehead and huffed.

So far, on their second and last sales excursion, they'd visited five stores. Jojo had waited in the car, while Simon made sale after sale. She'd wanted to help, but she'd had more important things to think about. Chip had called her the day before and explained about his disappointing non–date with Leanne. Jojo felt like she was back to square one. She had to think of something else, some other way to help Leanne and bring her into their group.

Simon straightened his bow tie. "You don't exactly have the greatest attitude."

"Come on, Simon," Jojo replied. "I'm helping, aren't I?" She held up the program ad paperwork. She'd kept track of everything and drawn logos for each ad.

"At least you're doing something." Simon popped a stick of gum into his mouth. "The way you're dressed, you might as well hide in the trunk. You couldn't even sell a mint Ty Cobb baseball card dressed like that."

Jojo *had* dressed down. Hair in her face. Soggy black sweater. Black tights — complete with a large tear — and squeaky, wet tennis shoes. "Appearances don't matter," she said.

"Right." Simon frowned at her. "You should have stayed at school and gone to the talent show rehearsal, your act is so good. Hey, maybe you should be in the show this Wednesday."

"What are you talking about, Simon?"

He thought for a minute, then tapped the window. "Never mind. Look, we only have to sell one more ad, and then we've got to get back to school and turn this stuff in so they can print the program in time for the show. I'm sick of doing all the work. Why don't *you* go into Sellman's Jewelry Store?"

"Fine," Jojo agreed without hesitating. Maybe she was dragging her feet on this project, but in the past she'd worked harder than anyone raising money for her school. "I will!"

She hopped out of Simon's car and slammed the door. After a few sloshy steps, she pushed her way into Mr. Sellman's sparkly clean shop. She'd met Mr. Sellman at one of her parents' parties, and luckily he was there, waiting on two college students who were picking out wedding rings.

Jojo look over the diamond necklaces and smiled. "Hi."

Mr. Sellman glanced up for the briefest moment. He quickly stowed some rings under the counter, then looked away again.

Jojo tapped the glass counter. She tried to get Mr. Sellman's attention again, but he didn't seem to recognize her. So she stood, leaning over rows of watches and rings. She stood, and stood. Finally Mr. Sellman glanced at her again, then whispered something to his assistant.

Jojo tried to smile again, but this time her

mouth wouldn't move. This was no conscious effort to look moody, but a deep, creepy feeling that she was not wanted. The assistant watched her hands, as if she were about to shoplift. Jojo's every move seemed to create suspicion.

"Can you help me?" Jojo finally asked.

"I know it's raining out, but you can't stay in here," the assistant stated. "This is a business, not a hang out."

"What?"

"I'm afraid you'll have to leave."

Jojo felt as if she'd been spat on. She wanted to scream, But this is me! Joanne Hernandez! Youngest daughter of Dr. and Mrs. Hernandez. You sold my parents my middle school graduation watch. All right, I'll go home and change. Then will you talk to me and stop acting like I'm some kind of thief? But she couldn't say anything, because Mr. Sellman's assistant was already guiding her by the elbow and leading her out the door. A moment later she was standing in the rain again, feeling cast off and dirty.

Jojo wished she could have beamed herself home, but the rain was really coming down and she had to drop the ad paperwork back at school. She had no choice but to get in Simon's car.

"What happened?" Simon asked as soon as she opened the door.

Jojo slid in and faced the window. "They weren't very supportive," she sighed.

"It looked to me like you didn't even push our product," Simon accused. "You barely talked to them."

She didn't want Simon to know how she'd been snubbed. Suddenly all she wanted was to change her clothes and go back to being the old Jojo. "One ad more or less won't matter. Oh, Simon, why don't you take me back to school right now so I can watch the end of the talent show rehearsal."

Simon didn't start the car. "Maybe it was your first impression. Maybe they thought you were like your homeless friend."

Jojo's stomach clenched. She had been thinking about Leanne with her platinum hair and bargain clothes. She wondered if everyone looked at Leanne the way Mr. Sellman's assistant had just looked at her. Leanne didn't have the luxury of going home and changing back into her cheerleading skirt. "That's exactly what they thought," she finally admitted in a quiet voice. "And they treated me like dirt."

Simon tapped the steering wheel. "That's a

drag, huh." He glanced at her. "No fun. I sure don't like it when people treat me like dirt."

"And what is that supposed to mean?

Simon shrugged and finally turned the key in the ignition. "Look, Jojo, I know I'm obnoxious. Everyone tells me so, not just you. I try too hard and then I act like a nerd. I know other high school kids don't appreciate me, but I'm just trying to do something in the real world. Okay?"

Jojo stared at the side of his freckled face. "It's okay, Simon," she sighed as they headed up Ocean Avenue. She was trying so hard to change and all she'd done was alter her outsides. But maybe the outside had finally taught her something. Maybe it was time to start looking in.

She gave Simon a sympathetic smile. "I'm glad I've been doing this with you. It's made me think about some important things."

He looked at her.

Jojo shrugged. "I'm sorry. All I want is to do something real, too."

"Lisa and Brandy asked us to make their spotlight really bright, Chip."

"I bet," Chip sighed. "Just how brightly lit do you think Brandy and Lisa want to be?"

"Bright enough so the audience won't look at anyone else."

Chip shook his head. "If you've got it, you might as well flaunt it."

"Right."

"And if you flaunt it, you'd better have it."

Neither of them laughed.

While the rehearsal for the talent show was taking place on the Crescent Bay High stage, Gabe and Chip were in the back of the auditorium, sorting through wires and cables. Gabe had volunteered to set up the lights, while Kat schlumped through both parts of their emcee routines in her rubber rain boots and an overall jumper. He'd intentionally avoided rehearsing with her. Because part of him wanted to flaunt something, too. But he wasn't sure if he had anything to flaunt. He didn't know whether he and Kat had something new and spectacular, or if it was still the same old Gabe and Kat show.

"Chip, I need your advice," Gabe said in a soft voice. There was the constant rattle of the rain on the auditorium roof and the occasional twang of a musical instrument warming up backstage.

"You're the one who knows about lights and electrics," Chip tossed back. "I'm just trying to be useful, and keep my mind off this whole mess with Leanne."

"That's not what I mean," Gabe explained. He dropped the piece of lighting gel he was trimming and stared up at the stage. Sam Stein was going through a fairly bizarre routine, pretending to be the inside of a gym locker, smothering under a pile of dirty clothes. Miranda, Jojo, plus teachers and class officers were sitting in the first few rows laughing their heads off. "I need personal advice," Gabe whispered.

"Not from me you don't," Chip sighed. He sat back on the floor, put on his glasses, and took a swig of carrot juice. He handed the container to Gabe.

"No, thanks." Kat stepped onto the stage after Sam pretended to die after being choked by his socks. For a moment Kat seemed to look right at Gabe and a wave of electricity flowed through him, as if all the cords and wires around him had been plugged in. But then Kat grinned at the small audience instead and cracked a joke. Gabe couldn't laugh. Not at their routines. Not at their eternal palsy relationship. And certainly not at the way he was no longer able to keep up the old Gabe Sachs macho bluff and turn this whole thing into a joke.

When Kat had kissed him, it had been like a gigantic key had gone inside and cracked open his heart. Somewhere inside a giant YES had escaped, a big, uncontrollable voice that screamed, Kat. *KAT!* My God, has it been Kat all along? My best buddy, sister, and friend? Was she the reason I never wanted to do more than flirt? Was she the reason I never let things get heavy with any other girl?

"Gabe, you're the expert with girls," Chip mumbled.

"I'm the expert in getting things started with girls," Gabe admitted. He put the lighting filter down and sat back. "But how do you take that next step? That's a whole new thing to me."

"I've tried to take the next step with every girl I've liked," Chip said. "And this thing with Leanne feels new to me, too. I don't know what's going on with her."

Gabe had to wonder what was going on with Kat, too. After Kat had kissed him, she'd just given him a funny look, as if the whole thing had been some kind of accident — like their lips had accidentally been in the same air space at the same time. He'd been left like a rag doll, stunned to the core of his being, while she'd ambled off to keep dancing with other guys. He'd almost had the feeling that the kiss was part of some other agenda, that it had had more to do with some weird quirk in Kat than an overwhelming desire for him.

"I wonder how many times a guy can get dumped," Chip muttered, "before he finally just gives up."

"I wonder if two people who are just friends for a long time can ever turn it into anything else," Gabe said.

Chip coiled some cable around his knuckles, then rapped his fist against the floor. "I keep telling myself that Leanne must have had a good reason for standing me up. But then I realize that I don't care if Leanne had the best reason in the world. She still should have talked to me when I called her. I wouldn't have done that to anyone."

Gabe nodded. "I know."

"The weirdest part is that I don't feel just hurt and bummed, like I usually do when this kind of stuff happens," Chip confessed. "I don't even feel optimistic. I feel different. I feel like I've never felt before."

"Tell me about it," Gabe agreed.

"I'm mad," Chip admitted. He turned to

Gabe. "I'm really mad. It's like there's this Chip inside me that was mad a million times before and didn't know it, and now that Chip is finally coming out."

But Gabe had to wonder if a new Gabe wasn't popping out, too. Or a new Kat? But he couldn't think about it much longer, because he heard footsteps scurrying up the aisle and a moment later he saw Miranda hurrying toward them in her jumper and riding boots, her long hair clipped back on either side and a pencil behind her ear.

Miranda leaned over the back row. "Chip, do you know where Leanne is? Her song is next. If she doesn't show up at this rehearsal, she's cut from the show. That's the rule."

"I'm not the one to ask about Leanne," Chip answered in a gloomy voice.

"I'm going to have to cut her song," Miranda explained. "There's nothing else I can do."

Miranda was about to rush back to her seat when the back door to the auditorium swung open. Brent Tucker stuck his head in, then sauntered through the door, wearing loafers, pleated slacks, and a tan raincoat over an oxford cloth shirt so crisp you could break it like a potato chip.

Miranda froze. "Are you working on the talent show, Brent?"

"What?" Brent looked around the auditorium. First his eyes settled on Kat, who was introducing the next number. Then he took in Chip and Gabe. Finally he looked at Miranda again with a charming, dimpled smile. "Oh, yeah. Of course. I came by to see what I could do to help. I just want to get involved."

"That's nice." Miranda stared back at him, rocking a little on her riding boots as if Brent made even her nervous. "I have to go back and watch the rehearsal. Maybe Gabe and Chip can find something for you to do." She gave a last wary glance at Brent, then rushed down the aisle again.

Gabe picked up a small wire cutter and tossed it up and down in his palm. Of course he'd seen Kat dancing with Brent at the spirit dance. He couldn't have missed it if he'd been blindfolded. Kat had assured him that she was through with Brent, but he had to face the fact that Brent was back in the equation after all.

"Well, well," Brent sang. As soon as Miranda was gone, his whole demeanor changed. His mouth tightened, and his dimples disappeared. He leaned with his back against the last row of chairs and concentrated on Gabe and Chip. "So good to see you, guys."

"Same to you, Tucker," Gabe growled. He'd hated Brent from the moment he'd met him. But most people thought that Brent Tucker was the best thing to hit Crescent Bay since sunshine. So far Brent had fooled most of the school with his clever Boy Scout act, but Gabe saw the naked ruthlessness in Brent's eyes.

Chip took off his glasses as if he were seeing it, too.

"I'm sick of your crowd," Brent said in a low voice.

Gabe was surprised by Brent's bluntness. "Am I supposed to break down and cry?"

"You guys don't like me," Brent explained. "And I certainly don't like you."

"What about it?"

"I'm just trying to figure out what to do," Brent said with a smug smile. "That's all."

Gabe and Chip looked at one another.

"I figure, there are some people you need to keep on your side." Brent looked over his shoulder again, this time focusing on Miranda. "And there are some people you just give up on. And when you decide you've had enough, the only thing to do is declare out-and-out war."

"What are you talking about, Tucker?" Chip asked, with surprising force.

Brent pointed at Gabe. "You tell Kat she can't hide from me by throwing herself at you." Then he turned to Chip. "And you tell Leanne that going out with you cost her her job."

"What?" Chip cried.

Brent smiled. "That's what I think of your crummy little crowd. And I'll tell you something else. All of you had better think twice about the way you've been treating me. Because I can make all your lives miserable, if I really want to." Brent cast one more look toward Kat and Miranda, then strode back out.

Chip jumped to his feet even as the door was swinging shut.

Gabe didn't want to think about what Brent had just said. Kat was just hiding from Brent? Kat had kissed him only to keep Brent at bay? The idea of Kat using him that way made Gabe sick to his stomach.

Gabe clambered up after Chip, catching him before he reopened the door. "I bet that's why Leanne didn't show up at the club, Chip. She was freaked because Tucker got her fired."

"Maybe you're right," Chip said, staring after

Brent with a fierce expression. "All I know is that I'm suddenly so angry at everyone and I'm not sure what I'm supposed to do."

"I know what you mean," Gabe breathed. "I've had about enough of this, too."

THIRTEEN

"*May I have your attention please.*"

Everyone in Leanne's homeroom glanced up as Vice Principal Hud's voice blasted over the intercom.

"*The entire student body will report to the auditorium during seventh period for the spirit talent show today. Students will go to their seventh-period classes first, then walk over to the auditorium in an orderly manner. You are being excused from class to appreciate the talents of your fellow Sea Lions. Anyone caught wandering around during the talent show or trying to leave campus will be punished.*"

"You tell us, Hud."

"Oh, Huuuuuddy."

"Big Hud is watching you."

The homeroom teacher shushed the class as Mr. Hud's voice crackled the speaker again.

"*Talent show participants will be excused from*

sixth-period classes as well. But they must have passes. And they must spend that free period in the auditorium getting ready for the show."

"Lighten up, Dud."

"What does he think we're going to do?" asked a drama student who was in the show. "Leave the school and go surfing? We need to prepare."

"I've heard the talent show is really going to be wild this year."

"I heard it's pretty different this time. People are doing some really far-out stuff."

"I heard that, too. Two really funky guys in my gym class are doing this magic act, and Carin Baker is doing some mime thing."

"No!!! I can't wait."

Leanne sank down in her seat as the chatter continued. Talent show, talent show. This number, that act. Since she'd arrived at school that day everyone had been talking about it as if it were the Academy Awards.

Leanne couldn't face it. Instead of a sixth-period excused slip, she'd gotten a note informing her that "Saturday's Girl" had been cut from the show. Big deal. Leanne had known when she skipped rehearsal that that would be the end of it. Just like she'd known when she'd skipped the Lara O'Toole concert, that would be the end of her and Chip.

Still, Leanne didn't think she could face watching Lisa and Brandy's dance number or the rest of the show. Just like she couldn't face Chip again. Not that she didn't like Chip. Maybe she liked him too much — way too much — which was why she couldn't look at his sweet, hopeful face. Her world wasn't sweet. Her world wasn't hopeful. Her world was a place with no job, no friends, and no family. It was a place where nothing panned out, where she was quickly running out of rent money, and soon would have no place to live.

As soon as the bell went off, Leanne shot to her feet, planning concrete ways to avoid the talent show that afternoon. She could fake an illness. She could leave a note on the activities bulletin board, asking to meet some peer counselor with Friends in Need. Or she could just sneak off campus. Even if Hud was sniffing the corridors like a bloodhound, she could probably evade him and get away. Plans to avoid Chip would be more difficult. The talent show would soon be over, but Chip would be at Crescent Bay High every day forever more. In a few days,

she would certainly run into him in the library
or the quad.

As Leanne hurried down the crowded hall, she
realized that she would run into Chip even
sooner than that. He was heading right for her.
Everything about him looked different. His
glasses were on. He held his backpack tightly
across one shoulder. He walked in his sandals as
if they were athletic shoes with cleats.

As soon as Leanne saw him, she turned and
walked the other way. Maybe he'd follow her
for a while, but she wouldn't slow down this
time. Eventually, he'd get her message. No matter how nice you are to me, it won't make any
difference. I don't deserve it. And I don't care
about your friends, your deals, or your overly
sweet concern.

As she moved even faster, she heard him calling out to her. He was a little out of breath,
pushing his way through the crowd.

"Leanne, I want to talk to you!" Chip projected.

Leanne was surprised by the force in his voice.
But she didn't stop. She began to jog, weaving
around people and locker doors until Chip cor-
nered her outside the music room. She spun

around and said, "Look, I'm sorry I didn't show up for the Lara O'Toole concert, but something came up."

"Something came up?" he repeated. He shook his head, and his hair swung across his face.

"I was in a bad mood," she challenged, trying to pretend that she didn't care. "I guess it was just bad timing . . . bad luck."

"Bad luck?" he repeated.

"That's what I said. Bad luck." She glared, expecting him to wilt and fade away. But he didn't. He just stood there, his eyes becoming furious. Suddenly she was the one who wanted to wilt and fade away. Desperate to get away from him, she turned and pushed her way into the girls' bathroom.

There were six or seven girls inside busily primping between classes. Leanne had just settled into the cool tiled corner, crouching away from the perfume and the smoke, when the bathroom door opened again and Chip walked in.

Leanne stared at him, unable to believe her eyes. "What are you doing?"

The other girls cowered, giggled, and shrieked.

Chip glanced around and blushed, but refused to leave. "Bad luck, huh? I'm sick of all this talk about luck," he said to Leanne. "Sure, you've had bad luck, but that isn't all of it. Standing me up wasn't bad luck." He raised his voice. "Not for you, anyway!"

"Don't yell," Leanne pleaded. The other girls were still giggling and staring away. "And you're not supposed to be in here."

"I think it's about time I yelled for a change!" Chip exploded. "And I don't care what I'm supposed to do. I'm sick of being so understanding and nice. I used to think it wouldn't matter how many times I got dumped on, because I could just count to ten and start all over again. Well, I can't do that anymore. I'm too angry, and I'm too hurt."

Leanne could barely look at him. "That's not my fault."

"Yes it is," he cried. "I know why you didn't show up at the club Saturday night. I'm sure it wasn't your fault that Brent Tucker got you fired from your job. And it wasn't your fault that those girls laughed at you when you tried out for the talent show. And it's not your fault that your mother's boyfriend is a jerk. But it was your fault that you stood me up. It was your fault when you wouldn't answer my phone call. It was your fault when you didn't show up for the talent show rehearsal and got cut from the show."

Leanne clutched her stomach. Her hands began to shake.

Chip backed up self-consciously, looking around at the other girls. "That's all I have to say. I'm sorry. Excuse me. I'll get out of here."

After Chip left, the giggling and gasping bubbled up again, but Leanne barely heard it. She was too full of Chip's words, which were playing over and over in her head.

By sixth period, everything was making Kat nervous. She was about to appear in front of the entire school. She'd wanted to rehearse with Gabe during lunch, but he'd avoided her. And Brent had left another note for her in the dressing room backstage. This note had definitely not contained a message of everlasting love.

Dear Kat: Go ahead. Kiss Gabe. Do your show. Don't forget me. I sure won't forget you. Or your friends. Not now. Not ever.

B.T.

"Look what you got, Kat!" exclaimed Carin

Baker, who was covering her face with white makeup.

"Are those for you, Kat?" Sam Stein had to know.

"Who are they from?" demanded Lisa Avery as she smoothed on another layer of lip gloss.

They were all huddled over their communal makeup counter, staring at the huge box of chocolate truffles that had been left with Brent's note. The candy was delicious, no doubt. Expensive, too. But to Kat, the white-and-gray box might as well have contained poisoned apples.

"The truffles are from my parents," Kat lied. "Help yourself. I don't want any. I'm too nervous to eat."

The rest of the cast descended like vultures, devouring the rich candy in minutes and then jumping up and down, joking about their sugar highs. It was already chaos. Singers were warming up. Juggling balls were flying. Miranda and the rest of the planning committee were running around like maniacs. Chip was pounding a hammer, doing last-minute work somewhere on stage. And Gabe was somewhere . . . doing something. All Kat knew was that he wasn't backstage with her, going over their routine. If he didn't show up soon, she was going to jump out of her skin.

Kat looked over her routine notes on three-by-five cards, then took deep breaths. Finally she stood on tiptoe to search for Gabe again. Instead she spotted Jojo, peeking in the dressing room door, looking so different that Kat wondered if Jojo were in costume, too. Then Kat realized that Jojo just looked like her old normal self again, in a yellow pleated skirt with a matching polo shirt and pink sweater. Jojo was carrying a foil balloon. She squeezed through the crowd and handed it to Kat.

"Here. I brought you this. It's for luck," Jojo said. "I realized that I was kind of ignoring the fact that you were in this show. I wanted to do something."

"Thanks." Kat clung to her. "I'm glad to see you. Really glad. You look nice."

Jojo glanced down at her clothes. "I don't know how I look or what it means. I know I've been kind of weird the last couple of weeks, since my party. Not that I feel like the old Jojo. Anyway, I just came to wish you good luck, or break a leg, or whatever it is I'm supposed to say."

"Thanks. I appreciate it." Kat hugged Jojo. "Don't worry about being weird. As far as I'm concerned, weirdness is a way of life." Kat searched for Gabe again. That nervousness was still deep in her stomach, making her feel almost sick. She tugged Jojo's sleeve. "Jo, don't let Hud catch you without a pass."

"Mrs. Sale thought I was in the show, and she gave me a slip." Jojo waved her pink paper.

"Good." Kat took a deep breath. "Have you seen Gabe?"

Jojo nodded. "I saw him on my way in here. He's sitting in the hall by himself. I didn't want to bug him. I thought he was going over his lines."

"Considering that all his lines depend on my lines, I'd say he's a guy that needs to be bugged." Kat crumpled Brent's note and threw it into the trash. She hugged Jojo again. "Thanks for the balloon. I've got to find Gabe. If we don't go over our opening routine I'm going to run away and join the Marines."

Kat hurried past the door that led to the costume storage room and rushed around the side of the auditorium. She found Gabe just where Jojo said he would be, sitting in the hallway in front of a row of lockers. He was in his usual dark jeans and T-shirt, his arms folded and his face resting on his arms.

Kat plopped down right next to him. "Gabe, remember me? Kat McDonough, also known as Patty Prom Queen, Miss Grundy, and countless other characters that make up my multiple personality."

He turned away. "Don't remind me."

"Gabe, what's bugging you?"

"What's bugging me, is what's bugging you," he answered.

Kat knew perfectly well what was bugging both of them. Okay, so she'd kissed him recklessly, thoughtlessly. She hadn't planned to do it. She'd even liked it. A lot. But she didn't want to think about what it meant or where they were supposed to go from here. After everything she'd been through with Brent, the last thing she was ready for was thinking about some intense romance with her best buddy, Gabe. For once, the idea of a kiss with no strings attached appealed to her. Just a little spark that didn't have to turn into a major fireworks display — at least not right now. She thought that Gabe — the champion of flirting — would understand that.

She grabbed Gabe's sleeve. "Can we at least go over our opening routine? Are we going to do the car mechanic characters or not?"

He would barely look at her. "I don't know."

"Gabe, we have to decide. I don't want to improvise everything."

"Why not?" Gabe shot back. "It seems to me that you do a lot of things without thinking these days."

Kat flinched. "You should know. Anyway, I'm not up for too many more surprises. I just want this talent show to go well and for our routine to go smoothly."

Gabe just stared down at his hands, refusing to reply to her until they both heard sharp footsteps and looked up to see Mr. Hud patroling the hall. Hud marched down to them with military precision. Hands behind his back, his eyes lingered on the pair of them. Kat clammed up and put on her most innocent smile.

"Do you two have passes?" Mr. Hud asked.

"Yes, sir," Kat barked. Then she started to giggle, the way she had in Hud's office. She looked to Gabe, but he was serious as a post.

"I just saw someone walking around here," Mr. Hud informed them. He rubbed his bald head and looked up and down the hall. "He looked like he wasn't really part of things, but was just looking for trouble."

Kat stiffened. She inched closer to Gabe as her nerves turned to cold fear. "Oh. Did you see who it was?"

"No," Mr. Hud growled. "But I'll find out."

The VP marched off, and Kat began to tremble. She leaned against Gabe's arm, trying to get closer to his comforting, familiar warmth. She nudged Gabe. "Between Hud and this show, I think I'm frozen with nerves. Do you want to help warm me up?"

"I'm not your protector," Gabe said. He stood up. "If you want to get rid of Brent Tucker, you'd better leave me out of it."

Kat's eyes opened wider. She reached for Gabe's hand, but he moved too quickly for her and soon she was grasping nothing but air.

Miranda had checked off everything on her list. Everyone in the cast had arrived. Instruments, tap shoes, props, all of it was there. Andrea had all her piano music. The seventh-period bell would ring in ten minutes. They were ready to go.

Miranda was ready, too. She was standing by the main door, as if she were waiting to usher in the first group of kids. Of course, that wasn't what she was doing at all. She was hoping to run into Jackson, who was bringing the programs over from the newspaper room. When she'd run into him on the quad, she'd had an even stronger sense of how much was still unfinished between them. She wanted to say, See? I did it. The talent show isn't going to be like it was last year. I don't shudder when Greg Brett's band plays those strange songs they wrote. I don't cringe when the girl with the pink hair does her monologue. I'm not afraid of taking chances or stuck in some outmoded set of rules.

She heard footsteps coming down the hall and quickly turned, hoping to see Jackson's dark hair and eager, curious eyes. But she didn't see anyone and for a moment she was confused. She looked up and down the corridor again, wondering if someone had slipped up the stairs or snuck into the bathroom. Then she felt a light tap on her shoulder, and she let out an involuntary cry.

"Ah!"

"Hello."

"Yes?"

"Miranda?"

"What?" Miranda spun around, her heart was going double time.

"Can I talk to you?"

It was Leanne Heard, with her dark red mouth, high heels, and thrift-store dress.

"Oh, hello," Miranda said. "What is it?"

Leanne thought for a moment, then took a deep breath. "Look, I know it's probably impossible. I don't have a pass, and I cut class to come here. But I want to be in the show. I have to do it. Is there any way you can put me back in so I can do my song?"

Miranda saw the need and courage on Leanne's face, but it was too late to make a change. "Leanne, the rule is that if you didn't show up at the rehearsal, you can't be in the show."

"I know I can do the song," Leanne persisted. "Don't you understand how important this is to me?"

"But the program has been printed. The rules . . ."

That was when Miranda heard footsteps again. Purposeful footsteps this time, not someone sneaking around. A moment later Jackson appeared with his arm full of programs. He stalled, looking back and forth between Miranda and Leanne.

Leanne shook her head and started to leave.

Miranda reached out to her. "Leanne, I'll

make an exception for you and let you back in the show," she said in a bold voice. She glanced back at Jackson. "If anyone gives you a hard time, you tell them to talk to me about it. You'd better grab Andrea and go over your song. You'll be right after Lisa and Brandy's dance."

Leanne closed her eyes if she were saying a prayer, backed up three steps, turned around twice, and then strode quickly into the auditorium.

FOURTEEN

"Some people are such fools," Brent Tucker swore.

He was still hidden in the stairwell after the flood of students had marched down — side by side, class by class — to the auditorium for the talent show. Not Brent. He didn't march. He didn't wait for a hall pass, stand in line, take his seat quietly, or raise his hand.

Brent had actually been cutting class since lunch, roaming around, checking out every inch of the auditorium and the surrounding halls. He'd forged an excuse on Tucker Resort stationery, just in case he got caught. But he wasn't going to get caught. Vice Principal Hud wasn't even worth worrying about. He strutted up and down the halls in his wing tips, making so much noise that he might as well have announced himself with a ten-gun salute.

Now Brent tread silently. He knew when to move and when to hold his ground. Since the end of sixth period he hadn't budged from his favorite spying place — the crook of the stairwell, ten steps up from the auditorium's main doors. From there, he'd looked down on Miranda. He'd watched her checking off names on her clipboard, while clearly being preoccupied with something else. He'd seen Leanne show up, too.

Actually, spying on Miranda and Leanne together had started to fill the void left by Kat's rejection. Miranda and Leanne: the high road and the low. One was the control queen who needed to get down, and the other a rebellious outsider who needed to climb up. Brent had been working on Leanne since he'd arrived in Crescent Bay, but Miranda . . . she was the one girl in that crowd he'd never laid a finger on, which suddenly made her the only one worth his time.

A ringing of microphone feedback echoed inside the auditorium. Brent cocked an ear as Roslyn Griff, the student body president, spoke over the PA.

"Now that everyone is settled, let's get started," Roslyn announced. "I would like to introduce our mistress and master of ceremonies for this year's spirit talent show. They're the team you all know from Totally Hot, their famous radio show on KHOT, our campus station. Welcome, Kat McDonouuuuugh and Gaaaaaabe Sachs!"

Hearing Kat's name still made Brent's muscles clench, but he forced himself to relax. He wanted to put his Kat obsession behind him. He wanted to do something so bold, so definitive that he would purge himself of his feelings once and for all.

Not making a sound, Brent crept down the stairs. As applause welcomed Kat and Gabe onto the stage, Brent surveyed the scene from his vantage point. The hall was empty, but Hud and two teachers stood guarding the auditorium doors. All three of them were watching the show, arms folded while leaning in the doorways. Brent figured that a few more teachers would be stationed in the foyer. The rest would be scattered throughout the auditorium, either pacing the aisles or watching the side doors.

Brent stood silently. He listened to the beginning of the show knowing that he would wait for his opportunity. He wasn't sure what that opportunity would bring, but he knew that it would come. And when it did, he would do something effective, powerful, and painless . . . for him.

"Now I've heard that we have some unusual talent numbers this year," said Kat, as flirty Patty Prom Queen. "I've always said, what's the point of doing a number if it's not unusual."

The flirtiness in her voice made Brent's stomach churn.

But Gabe, as Larry Lounge Lizard, sounded surprisingly cool. "Just don't do a number on me, Patty."

"On you?" Kat sounded a little flustered. "Who said you were talented?"

"What is talent?"

"What is unusual?"

"What is what?"

"What?"

"Never mind. Now for our first act . . ."

There'd been a missed beat, an awkward laugh. The chemistry they'd displayed at the spirit dance was missing. Brent wondered if something was off between Kat and Gabe or if it was just nerves.

"Who cares anymore," he grunted. He still couldn't believe how Kat had gotten to him. Kat should have been writing *him* notes and pining away, not the other way around. Now all Brent wanted was revenge.

Brent waited patiently in the hall. While one talent act blurred into the next, he considered his possibilities. If he could only get inside the foyer and into the back of the auditorium, he could attack the fuse box and plunge Kat and Gabe into darkness. Or, if he really hurried, he could race out in his BMW, buy some kind of a stink bomb, and lob it from the balcony. He could even do more graffiti in the auditorium foyer.

"Think," he told himself. "Maneuver. Plan."

Brent knew that he could only get away with those acts if Hud and the teachers abandoned their posts. No matter how much Brent yearned to screw up Kat's beloved talent show, he would only make his move if he knew he wouldn't get caught.

So he continued to wait as students guffawed at Sam Stein. They sat silently for Carin Baker's mime routine, until taped music blared for Lisa and Brandy's dance number.

Finally Mr. Hud and the teachers abandoned their hall post. They wandered into the auditorium for a better view of the show, and Brent crept closer so that he could see, too.

Brandy and Lisa were kicking and wiggling with shapely legs and slick smiles. The rest of the school was bowled over by them, but Brent was bored. His interest wasn't roused until the pair left the stage and Kat stuck her head out again, waving a piece of paper.

"Last-minute bulletin. Just in!" Kat cried. She blew the whistle hanging from the cord around her neck. "There's going to be a change in the program. Instead of Jane Flash going next, we're going to squeeze in a solo singer. This time it will be junior Leanne Heard, singing "Saturday's Girl.""

Brent wasn't sure why there had to be a special announcement just for Leanne, but whatever the reason, it couldn't have suited him more perfectly. The announcement of Leanne's name had a definite effect on the crowd. Whispers fluttered back and forth. Giggles erupted, and heads began to turn. As the ruckus began to swell, Hud nodded to the other teachers. They finally abandoned their posts and began to march up the aisles, glaring at gigglers, snapping fingers, and making threats.

"Well, well," Brent snickered.

He made his move. Completely unnoticed, he

snuck through the foyer and into the back of the
auditorium. First he saw Chip, who sat alone
against the back wall, operating the spotlight.
Brent didn't work too hard at evading Chip. He
didn't need to. As soon as Leanne stepped onto
the stage, Chip's whole body lurched forward.
As long as Leanne was on the stage, Chip
wouldn't have noticed if Brent had dropped a
bucket of water on his head.

Brent stood only a few feet from Chip while
Leanne launched into her song. Leanne wasn't
bad. Her voice was husky and musical, and she
had a definite sexy presence and grace. But Brent
wasn't about to stick around writing Leanne's
glowing review. He was moving again, because
he'd just spied the perfect revenge. It was waiting
by the emergency exit, and Brent wasn't about
to waste any more time.

Chip had heard something — a nearby foot-
step, an eerie scratching sound — but he
couldn't worry about it. All of his attention was
on Leanne. All of his warmth, his love, his optimism, and his luck was going out to her.

And why shouldn't it? Even though the audience was still a little restless, she was singing
with commitment and strength. When Leanne
snapped her fingers, and swayed to the music

Andrea played, the scoffing and smirking from the audience started to turn to interest and respect. Chip began to relax, too, so much that he even glanced around the back of the auditorium.

And that was when he saw the crack of light come in as someone opened the back emergency door.

Chip wanted to scream, "WAIT! STOP! NOOOOO!" But it all happened too quickly. Brent Tucker's hand went up, and Chip saw him smile. A second later, just as Leanne was launching into her second verse, the fire alarm went off.

It was instant panic. Leanne froze, her face full of pain, as if people had suddenly thrown things at her. The talk started again. People stood up in their seats and began to move toward the aisles. Teachers opened doors. Mr. Hud had found a bullhorn and was giving instructions. Through it all, Chip tried to make his way to the stage. He wanted to get to Leanne. But there were too many people. Too much chaos. Too much noise.

"Talk about an electrifying performance," one girl scoffed.

"Maybe we should start calling her Firestarter," said another.

Talk, talk. Name-calling and giggles.

The alarm was still blaring and making Chip's head spin. Now his anger burned inside. It sent Chip flying away from the crowd filing out of the auditorium. As soon as he was outside, he took off searching the halls until he caught a glimpse of Brent, who was jogging across the quad.

Chip didn't lose him. He darted down halls and across the football field. He ran recklessly, jumping over bushes and almost knocking down a custodian until he caught up with Brent in the student parking lot. Brent was climbing into his new BMW, looking disgustingly smug.

Chip grabbed Brent before he could get into the car. "Where do you think you're going?" he panted.

Brent pried Chip's hands away, then brushed himself off as if removing dirt. "I'm going home, wimp. You should, too, or maybe you should go back to your girlfriend. She'll probably need some comfort after the week she's had."

"You scumbag!" Chip raged. "How could you do that to Leanne? Don't you know what it meant for her to get up in front of everyone?"

Brent broke away from him for a split second and looked over Chip's shoulder, as if he were suddenly thinking about something else. Then he came back to Chip and shifted his stance. "You're really mad, aren't you, wimp?" Brent dared. "So why don't you hit me? I hurt your slutty little girlfriend, didn't I? So why don't you get me back?"

Chip knew he was being egged on. No matter how furious he was, he still didn't want to hit. He'd never been in a fight. Even as a kid, he'd always been able to talk it out and avoid punches and brawls.

"What's the matter?" Brent growled. "Do I have to do something else to your lowlife girlfriend, or to somebody else in your precious crowd? Where's your nerve?"

"Fighting doesn't take nerve," Chip said.

Brent looked over Chip's shoulder again, then looked down, as if he were giving up. Just when Chip relaxed, Brent lunged in with a quick, hidden punch right into Chip's gut. The pain was so sharp and hard that it stopped Chip's breath and made him see little flashes of silver light. A sour taste came into Chip's mouth and something broke lose inside him. He formed a fist, and with all his rage, he swung his arm. He landed one solid punch, right in Brent's face.

Brent stumbled back. He touched his nose, his

eyes wide with shock. He didn't seem too badly
hurt, until he glanced over Chip's shoulder again
and then threw himself back against his car. He
began to moan and writhe as if he were about
to die.

Chip cradled his own fist, confused about how
he could have hurt Brent so badly. He was completely disoriented, wondering how he could
have lost his temper so completely, and why
Brent was putting on such an act. Then he turned
to see Mr. Hud racing across the parking lot,
heading right for them.

"FREEZE RIGHT THERE!" Mr. Hud demanded.

Chip didn't move. Brent continued to moan
and wail.

Hud raced over and stood between them. He
held up his hands to prevent more fighting, but
Chip kept staring at his fist, which throbbed and
stung.

"Sorry, sir," Brent answered, as soon as
Mr. Hud arrived. With amazing calm, he pulled
a note out of his pocket. "I have to leave early
for a doctor's appointment. Here's my excuse.
I was just leaving, going about my own business, when he ran out of the auditorium and
attacked me." Brent touched his nose and

managed to produce a few drops of blood.

Chip was so astounded by what Brent was doing that he couldn't even speak.

"What do you have to say for yourself, Kohler?" Mr. Hud demanded.

"He hit me first!" Chip finally said.

"Spare me the fiction," Hud barked. "I saw the whole thing. Kohler, I saw you running away from the auditorium. For all I know, you pulled the fire alarm. One thing I know for sure is that you threw a punch." He looked at both boys, then handed the excuse slip back to Brent. "Get to your doctor's appointment, Tucker."

While Brent got into his car, Chip turned to Hud, unable to believe what was happening. He took a breath and started to explain.

Hud stopped him. "Save it, Kohler. Don't bother with excuses. I want you in detention right now. You'll stay there until five o'clock today and then you're suspended all day tomorrow. I'll call your parents, and you can bet that we're all going to have a nice, long talk.

Chip felt the sting in his knuckles. The BMW pulled away, and Brent Tucker was gone.

FIFTEEN

By the end of the talent show, most people had already forgotten the fire drill. There were jokes about Mr. Hud having run toward the parking lot like he'd been in flames, but other than that, the auditorium backstage was a chorus of Good job, You were the best, and That was the greatest talent show ever.

Kat, Miranda, and Jojo hadn't forgotten, however. While Kat scrubbed off her makeup at the backstage sink, Miranda and Jojo were huddled on either side of her, talking in hushed voices. Meanwhile, kids changed out of their costumes, laughed, and congratulated each other. One musician shook up a can of soda and sprayed it all over himself.

"I thought I would die when that bell went off," Miranda whispered, inching even closer to

Kat. "I was afraid of something like that happening. I knew the whole show wasn't planned closely enough."

"It wasn't your fault," Kat said as she scrubbed her face with soap and water. She held her necklace to one side and leaned over the sink. "I was just glad that something worse didn't happen. I was so nervous."

"Maybe I shouldn't have stuck Leanne back in at the last minute," Miranda considered.

"Yes, you should have," Jojo insisted. "I was really glad you gave Leanne a second chance."

Miranda looked at Jojo's reflection in the mirror. "You mean that, Jo?"

Jojo thought for a moment, then nodded. "I think it was one of the bravest things you've done in your whole time as class president. I only wish I could do something like that."

"Really? Thanks." Miranda smiled. "Maybe Jackson's right. Maybe I do need to take more chances and do more things that are a little risky."

"I don't know about that." Kat shook out her swim team towel and patted her face. "The fire drill wasn't your fault, anyway. Someone just pulled the alarm."

"I felt so awful for Leanne." Jojo cringed and fluttered her fingers, which were coated with red-and-white spirit polish again. "Why didn't the bell go off during Brandy and Lisa's dance? How could someone have done that to Leanne?"

"Maybe the bell went off by accident," Kat decided. "Or maybe they forgot about the talent show and it was a real fire drill." She stared at her face, then reached into Jojo's purse and borrowed some lipstick. "But you have to hand it to Leanne. She got right back up there as soon as everybody came back in."

Jojo nodded.

Kat smeared on the lipstick, then tossed it back to Jojo. "When we all were backstage again, after the drill, I asked Leanne if she wanted to skip her song and go right to Jane Flash. I told her the fire drill was just bad luck, and she didn't have to go on again if she didn't want to."

"What did Leanne say?" Miranda asked.

"She said she was sick of bad luck, and she wanted to get back up there and finish," Kat answered. "There was no way she wanted to quit. I could tell that it was really important to her."

The three girls were quiet for a moment, while Sam Stein did an encore of his gym locker routine and the other drama students stamped their feet and hooted.

"Leanne's song was pretty good, too," Miranda finally said. "If you like Lara O'Toole."

They moved away from the sink and looked around. The backstage crowd was beginning to thin out. Some class officers were cleaning up, and Mr. Bishop was collecting costumes.

"Where's Leanne now?" Jojo asked.

"I don't know." Kat stood on her tiptoes to search for her. "The second after we finished the show, I saw Leanne running out of the auditorium as if she couldn't wait to get out of here. I guess she went right home."

The three girls exchanged glances, then strolled by the makeup area, which was now a mass of dirty paper towels, cotton balls, and empty cups. In the middle was the chocolate-stained box that had held Brent Tucker's present. As they passed the table, Kat picked up the box and stuffed it into the trash.

Jojo stopped at the auditorium's back door. "Where's Chip?"

"I didn't see him after the show at all," Kat suddenly realized. "Did either of you?"

"No." Jojo checked the hall. "I guess I'll go look for him now."

Miranda checked her watch and gestured back toward the stage. "I'd better help with the cleanup."

"Okay." Kat looked down toward the library. "I'll find Gabe then." She reached out to Jojo. "Thanks again for the balloon, Jo. I'll see you all at lunch tomorrow, if I don't see you before."

"Okay."

"You were great, Kat."

"Thanks, Miranda. Talk to you tonight."

Kat tugged at the towel around her neck and pressed her way through the remaining cast members and well-wishers that were gathered in the hall. She'd been wanting to find Gabe ever since the show had ended. There'd been no time to talk during the performance, because everything had been so hectic. And she and Gabe needed to talk. It wasn't so much that their routine had been off, but that every improvisation had had an edge to it. It hadn't just been the usual boy/girl teasing that was their trademark, but something deeper and more troubling.

Kat wedged her way through the crowd lingering in front of the auditorium, and then began searching the halls. She jogged upstairs and down, to the radio station and the gym. She finally found Gabe on the school front lawn, leaning against the Sea Lion statue. The statue had been decorated for the spirit drive with a red-and-white cape that fluttered in the breeze.

She jogged up to him. "Hi."

He glanced at her, then stared back while cars backed out, buses rumbled, and kids yelled back and forth.

"How'd you feel about the show?" she asked.

He shrugged.

"What are you doing?"

"Looking for Chip," Gabe answered in a cool voice. "His van is still here, but I can't find him."

"Jojo went to look for him, too. Maybe he had to rush home for some reason."

"Without his van?"

"I see what you mean." Kat took a deep breath. She hated it when she and Gabe had these conversations where nothing connected. It was like having a best friend who suddenly didn't speak English, instead of having a twin who shared every inside joke. "I hope Chip didn't get sick. Maybe he went somewhere with Leanne. She left right after the show."

"Maybe he did."

Kat stood next to him for a while, watching the buses and feeling the comfort of being close to him, even though he was pretending that she wasn't there. It was more than comfort, she realized. But she didn't want to think about what her feelings really were or what they could become. Finally she nudged him. When he still didn't react, she slung her swim towel around his neck.

Gabe whipped off the towel and threw it back to her.

It was too much; Kat had to tell him. "Gabe! I don't want to start this," she cried. "I know I've been giving you mixed signals lately, and maybe it hasn't been very fair. All I know is that I can't handle it if you and I are on the outs again."

Gabe let out a long, deep sigh. "Look, Kat. I don't want to fight with you, either. I don't want to cancel our show, or our friendship, or . . . whatever it is that we have going. I just don't want you to play games with me."

Gabe really looked at her. For the first time Kat really admitted to herself that something between them had changed. She wasn't sure how or when it had happened, but there was something more than just friendship going on, and she wasn't sure what to do about it.

"Kat," he said in a serious voice. "Maybe I have no right to tell you to be straight with me, since I led so many girls on. But you're not other girls. Don't kid a kidder, because I know all the moves."

Kat almost stopped breathing for a moment. She knew what he was trying to say. After flirting with five hundred girls, Gabe was ready for a change. He was ready to take her seriously. But she had just gotten over Brent Tucker. Before that she'd had to get over a disastrous summer romance. She'd given up on guys, then thrown herself overboard. She had a lot of screaming and kicking and stretching and figuring out to do. Maybe Gabe was the one. *Maybe.* But she wasn't ready to settle down yet.

Or was she?

They both looked at each other, but for once neither one of them said a word.

Leanne sat near her secret lunch place, even though school had been out for two hours. She didn't mind. Time moved quickly because she had a lot to think back on, a lot to look forward to, and a lot of current problems to mull over and solve.

But as soon as the door to the detention room cracked open, she stood up. Three boys and one girl came out first, all shuffling, looking defeated and surly. Chip was last. He was different. His sandals slapped against the floor with angry pride, and he held his fist against his chest as if it were in a sling.

Leanne walked slowly, intercepting Chip before he could head out to the quad.

He took a moment to register who she was. It was almost as if he'd been asleep. He even rubbed his eyes and brushed back his hair.

"You're still here," he said.

She nodded. "Jojo found out what happened from a teacher. She came to look for you. She couldn't get in to see you, but she saw me at my locker, so she told me that you were in detention. I've been waiting for two hours."

"You've been waiting here for two hours? For me?"

"More. What can I say. It's been a day of firsts for me."

"You can say that again." Chip shook out his fist and winced.

Leanne gazed up at him. "Jojo also heard from a teacher that you went after Brent Tucker."

Chip looked off at the quad.

"Was Brent the one who pulled the fire alarm?"

Chip finally nodded. "Nobody will believe it,

though," he explained. "Tucker has an excuse for everything. I didn't tell Mr. Hud that Brent had done it because I knew he wouldn't believe me. What would be the point?"

Leanne almost laughed, except that it was too painful. How many times had she given in because she knew there was no point in fighting for the truth. "I know how that goes."

He looked at her with deep respect. "I'll bet you do."

"Did you do it for me?" she asked, in her quietest voice.

"Partly. I did it for myself, too," Chip said. "Not the fighting part. I did that because Tucker punched me first, and I just lost it. I'm still not very proud of having hit him. But I went after him in the first place because I was tired of having people hurt me and then telling myself to count to ten and make it okay."

"But it wasn't you he hurt," Leanne pointed out. "It was me."

"Same thing."

"What do you mean?"

"Never mind." Chip looked away.

Leanne wanted him to continue his thought. For once she didn't want to back out or push him away. "You know what? I went back on," she told him. "After everyone came back from the fire drill, I got back onstage and I sang my song. I thought I just did that for me. But now I realized I did it partly for you, too."

"For me?"

"To prove that I didn't always have to give in to bad luck."

He reached for her hand.

Just the tips of their fingers touched, but it was so scary that it was like walking on a wire over Niagara Falls. "Not that it will change anything," she sighed. "My rent is due soon, and I already owe from last month. I picked up my final paycheck, but it won't be enough."

"What will you do?"

"Go back home, I guess."

"Is your mother's boyfriend still there?"

Leanne nodded.

"I don't want you to go back there."

"I don't want me to go back there, either," she echoed. "But you can only do so much in one day."

He stepped closer. "You can do a lot in one day, if you ask me."

Leanne put her hand to his cheek and drew a delicate line down the side of his face. He put his head on her shoulder and she kissed his cheek.

Chip turned toward her, dropped his backpack on the ground and pulled her in with one arm. She wasn't sure whether she kissed him, or he kissed her, but it didn't matter. A lot of things that she used to be afraid of didn't seem so dangerous anymore.

SIXTEEN

Miranda was always amazed that things could change so quickly. Crescent Bay High could be obsessed with football, and as soon as the season ended it was on to band tournaments and debates. Couples changed partners. Spats flared up even among Miranda's close friends, only to blow over in a week or two. Her own junior year had been a whirlwind. In such a short time she'd gone from having her whole life planned out to not knowing what each day would bring.

"I have changed, haven't I?" she said to herself, as she strolled onto campus Friday morning. The custodian was still sweeping the hall, pushing the old spirit drive decorations into piles to be tossed away.

Miranda quickly skirted across the new quad — which didn't even seem new anymore.

The grass was growing in. The walkway was already dotted with old candy wrappers and outdated excuse slips. As Miranda passed the cafeteria, she saw that every trace of Kat's graffiti was gone. Even the pristine, white brick of the new cafeteria was starting to look broken in.

Miranda ducked into the library hall, where kids were staring into lockers, cleaning out that week's worth of stuff, throwing away unfinished lunches and old tests. She took in their conversations as she passed by.

"Maybe the basketball team will finally win tonight?"

"Who cares about basketball anymore? All new movies are playing at the Crescent Bay mall."

"I'm tired of the mall. I heard there's a new underage club on the highway."

"Did you hear that Roslyn Griff got into Princeton? I wonder who'll be student body president after she graduates?"

The talent show and Leanne's song were old news now. Even the fact that Chip had been suspended the day before seemed to have traveled the halls and died down already. The gossip changed so fast that Miranda thought they should have posted it on the billboard near the stadium. Instead of announcing that week's dance or athletic event, it could just say:

Miranda and Jackson, most mismatched and mysterious couple, break up. Something is still going on between them, but it's hard to tell exactly what it is.

Leanne Heard dares to join talent show, holding her own with Lisa Avery and Brandy Kurtz.

Chip Kohler, nicest guy in the junior class, suspended for fighting. Is something going on between him and Leanne?

Check the board tomorrow for the next installment.

Having made herself smile, Miranda slipped her calendar out of her briefcase and turned the corner. She headed toward the guidance office to check her schedule on the activities bulletin board. Miranda checked the board often. Right away, she found the section entitled Friends in Need, the peer counseling program. She was still training as a peer counselor, and there would probably be another workshop coming up soon. Her heart pounded as she checked the schedule. Jackson was a peer counselor, too. Whenever the next workshop happened, she would see that daring look in his eyes, and feel that strong, electric pull she felt anytime they were in the same room.

As Miranda searched for her pen, she kept thinking about Jackson. Sometimes she thought that Jackson was right. She was rigid and afraid. But other times she thought, No! I'm the one who longs to take steps into the unknown. I'm the one who had the guts to leave Eric and disappoint my dad. I made it possible for Leanne to step onto the auditorium stage. In the end, I might even be more adventurous than you, Jackson.

She wanted to stop right there, to run up to the journalism room, where she would probably find Jackson, and confront him once and for all. She knew what she'd say, too. Stop giving me those dares and sad looks. Maybe it's you who's being chicken, since you won't try to get back together with me. Maybe you're the one who's stuck in a rut!

But before she could think any further, Miranda spotted a slip of paper taped over the Friends in Need section. The note was neatly folded, and addressed in an elegant hand.

"It's from Jackson," she said out loud. Finally. Maybe Jackson was finally acknowledging that she'd pushed herself far enough. She plucked the note off the board and, without hesitating, ripped it open and read.

> Dear Miranda:
>
> Will you meet me as my peer counselor? I need to talk to you. I'm messed up. This thing with Kat has made me do crazy things, think crazy thoughts. The only way back is to talk to someone.
>
> As a Friends in Need counselor, I know you have an oath of confidentiality. I depend on that. Please meet me. Alone. I'll leave you another note with the time and place.
>
> Think of me.
>
> Brent Tucker

Miranda's first reaction was to throw the note away. Brent was a threat to her crowd. Kat said so. Chip had finally told them all that Brent had pulled the fire alarm. Chip was sure of it, even though Chip doubted that anyone else would believe him.

A chill traveled down Miranda's spine as she stuck the note into the pocket of her blazer. But she knew she would be brave enough to meet him alone and straighten him out. She would be the one to make Brent Tucker change.

"One day sure can feel like a long time," Chip told Jojo before lunch. They were standing in front of her locker while she sorted through old invitations and notes. She was throwing most of them away. Her mirror was still up, however, and her pompoms were dangling from the side hooks.

"I missed you the whole day yesterday," Jojo said.

"Thanks." Chip tousled her curls, then looked up and down the hall. "Let's hope you weren't the only girl who missed me."

"Have you seen Leanne?" Jojo asked, tapping Leanne's locker, which was right next to hers.

"Not yet," Chip said eagerly. "Are you still going to ask her?"

Jojo bit her lip, checked her face in her locker mirror, then looked away. "Of course."

"And you're sure it's okay with your mom?"

"My mom," Jojo repeated. "Yeah. It took my poor mom about an hour to realize that I was serious and that this wasn't some kind of fad that I was going to get tired of in another week. But I just kept telling her, Mom, this is serious.

Mom, this is different. Mom! This isn't about
shoes or hair or dumb things like that. This is
real." Jojo smiled. "And she finally got it. My
mom finally looked at me in a different way."

Chip patted her.

Jojo touched her stomach. "I'm still nervous,
though. Maybe I'll just leave Leanne a note, asking her to meet us in the caf. Miranda, Kat, and
Gabe are waiting for us."

"Just wait for her here," Chip advised. "I
don't think Leanne is ready to eat with the rest
of us in the caf. Jo, you don't have to ask her if
you don't want to."

"I want to." Jojo checked the hall again. She
stamped her aerobic shoes. "Let's just think
about other things until she gets here. I'll think
about something else. Anything . . . except Simon Wheeldon."

"Okay." Chip thought about his suspension
from school. The day at home had been fairly
strange. He'd watched game shows and eaten
vegetable soup while his parents went to work.
It had been a weird kind of punishment, he'd
decided. For him, it actually *had* been unpleasant,
because he hadn't been able to see Leanne or his
friends, or go to his classes, most of which he
really liked. But he doubted that the other de-

tention kids got misty-eyed over missing environmental science or Spanish 3. Most of them had probably gotten into trouble for cutting in the first place.

Jojo drummed her fingernails against her locker door. "Were your parents pretty mad at you?"

"They weren't thrilled," Chip sighed. "You know how they feel about fighting. I explained what happened, and they believed me. Then they said if I got into any more trouble, they were, like, going to send me to military school."

"Really?"

"Not really, Jo. It was a joke." Chip thought for a minute. "At least I hope it was."

Jojo frowned.

"They were pretty cool." Chip smiled and nudged Jojo. His optimism was back, even though he knew he'd taken a bum rap and Brent had gotten off. He also knew that if he got caught doing anything wrong again, he would be in serious trouble.

But none of that mattered when Chip finally saw Leanne step out of the stairwell and appear in the hall. From the way Leanne moved down the hall, no one ever would have known that she'd done something remarkable only two days before. She slunk in her high heels, letting one flap as she walked. Her hair partly covered her face, and she wore something that looked like an old, black slip under a ratty fur jacket. Everything about her said, Look at me, and Don't you dare get too close, at the same time.

But Chip knew that he'd gotten a little bit close, and he only wanted to get closer. He hadn't seen Leanne since after the talent show, and he had to control his desire to run to her and kiss her in front of everyone.

Leanne stopped a few feet away from them. She offered Chip the tiniest glance, then dug her hands into her pockets.

"Hi." Jojo offered her old grin.

Leanne shrugged.

Chip touched Leanne's shoulder, and their eyes connected. After a quiet, dizzying moment, he gestured to Jojo. "Jo wants to ask you something, Leanne. Okay?"

Leanne didn't answer.

Jojo closed her eyes for a moment. Then she began to blab. "Okay. I know you probably don't want to do this, but Chip told me about the situation you're in. I mean, how you don't have a job now and you can't afford your rent and you don't want to go back home."

Leanne flinched.

"Don't get mad at Chip for telling me," Jojo insisted. "I pried it out of him. I've kind of been thinking about you a lot lately, and then when I saw you sing that song at the show, I thought about you even more. *And* about myself."

"Jojo, just come out with it," Chip begged.

Leanne hugged her jacket.

"Okay, it's like this," Jojo said. "I asked my mom, and she said it's okay. I mean, I had to talk to her a long time about it, but she finally agreed with me that it was a good idea."

Leane was clearly confused.

"Jojo, you're acting like somebody wound you up too tight," Chip said.

"I know, Chip. Not everyone is Mr. Mellow like you. This is hard. Things that are real are hard. Okay, Leanne, would you like to live with us . . . at my house, I mean? My sister is at college, so her room is free. It wouldn't be a permanent thing, just until you get enough money to do what you want."

"You're asking me to live with you!" Leanne gasped.

"Yeah," Jojo answered. "I guess I am."

Leanne just stood there for the longest time. She looked back and forth between Jojo and

Chip. She bit her lip and stared at the floor. Finally she looked up. "Um, well. I'll think about it, Jojo. Thanks, I guess. Um, I'll let you know."

"I'm serious, Leanne," Jojo insisted. "This is a real offer. I know there's a lot I don't know about you. And about myself. But maybe I'm finally ready to start learning."

Leanne glanced at Chip. His face was as hopeful as Jojo's was nervous. He smiled at her. Leanne couldn't help it. She felt a hint of hope again, even though it was mixed with that old fear that taking on anything new would just mean more disaster and pain.

Leanne reached for Chip's hand. She took in the eagerness in Jojo's eyes and the warmth in Chip's. She took a step closer to Chip. She wondered if getting any more involved with Chip and his crowd could finally chase her bad luck away for good.

Don't miss book #4 *Making Changes* in the sizzling series:

TOTALLY HOT!

Jojo Hernandez is sick and tired of being thought of as just another bubble-headed cheerleader. Even her friends don't take her seriously. But now she's interested in someone who thinks she's really deep (at least she *thinks* he does). He's smart, gorgeous, *and* one of her best friend's ex-flames!

Ladies' man Brent Tucker is determined to destroy Kat and her precious crowd because she rejected him. This time his target is Kat's best friend, class president Miranda Jamison. Miranda thinks she's about to become Brent's peer counselor. But Brent has some counseling of his own in store for Miranda.

Meanwhile, Chip continues to chase after loner Leanne Heard, and Gabe decides it's time to ask Kat out on an official "date."